DONOVAN & SON

THE 25TH ANNIVERSARY BILL DONOVAN NOVEL

MICHAEL JAHN

FIVE STAR
A part of Gale, Cengage Learning

GALE
CENGAGE Learning

Detroit • New York • San Francisco • New Haven, Conn • Waterville, Maine • London

GALE
CENGAGE Learning

LIBRARY OF CONGRESS CATALOGING-IN-PUBLICATION DATA

Jahn, Michael.
   Donovan & son : the 25th anniversary Bill Donovan novel / Michael Jahn. — 1st ed.
   p. cm.
   ISBN-13: 978-1-59414-266-6 (alk. paper)
   ISBN-10: 1-59414-266-1 (alk. paper)
   1. Donovan, Bill (Fictitious character)—Fiction. 2. Police—New York (State)—New York—Fiction. 3. Fathers and sons—Fiction.
I. Title.
PS3560.A35D66 2008
813'.54—dc22   2008026747

First Edition. First Printing: October 2008.
Published in 2008 in conjunction with Tekno Books and Ed Gorman.

for Darby Anne Jahn

THANKS AND GOODBYES

Thanks to my mother, Anne Jahn; uncle Barney Loughlin; cousins Mary Ellen, Beth, and Patricia and their families; my sons, David Jahn and Evan Jahn, and Evan's family; and friends Chris Bodkin, Stu Chapman, Richard Faust, Ed Gorman, Marty Greenberg, John Helfers, Laird Kelly, Lesley Knight, Patty McGregor, Bill Millard, Neil Osterweil, Joanne Reinhardt, Marcia Ringel, Ed Susman, Jill Taylor, Tom and Barbara Travis, Lauren Walker, and Bruce Sylvester, my Yankee "cousin" whose Shelter Island sailor ancestors surely canoodled with my Southampton baymen ancestors. And a long overdue crossed-oars salute to Sharon Wolin.

I have some sad farewells to those who have gone since the last time I honored loved ones lost: Marlene Aig, Steve Baron, Eric Horn, Marian Loughlin, Walter Wager, David Walley, and Don Zahner.

A tearful farewell to and final bottle of Schmidt's for the absolutely irreplaceable Sam from 114th Street, who never returned from his 30th mission.

Finally, many more sunny Sunday afternoons at Loughlin Vineyards, Meadow Croft, Sayville, N.Y., where much of this book was written.

1. HE SAID ONE WORD, "MERCURY," AND DIED

Deep in the Manhattan granite, the basement of Riverside University's library had a whiff of moist concrete from the walls and slowly rusting steel from the bookracks. There was a hint of leather and mold, and the Captain wondered how the university elders expected decades-old books, logs, ledgers, and research notes to further survive. Thinking of how the ancient and estimable institution above and around him let matters molder, he felt a certain absence of care.

Absent also was Patrick McGowan. The scientist whose whereabouts Donovan sought had disappeared suddenly twenty-one years earlier, amidst a brilliant career researching genes and their habits. There was neither fanfare nor encore.

Where in hell had the man gone? A Nobel Prize beckoned, Riverside's second, everyone said, yet McGowan faded off into the mist. All Donovan was able to find in the university archives was some very sketchy stuff . . . logs, lab notes, and scribbled marginal hopes and befuddlements. Only the topic was clear—how a codon or two, whatever they were, in the DNA flicked a switch in the RNA (and the difference between DNA and RNA was but vaguely clear to the Captain), and *that* had a role of one sort or other in the chain of events that turned plain-vanilla stem cells into nerve cells.

Donovan didn't particularly want to know how the goddam stuff worked. He wanted to find someone who *did*—and well enough to help find a cure for the paralysis that left his beloved young-old son, Danny, confined to a wheelchair unable to walk.

"Confined" was the wrong word, though. "Commanding" a wheelchair was more like it. All the while the famous NYPD detective (who had retired to a sort of consultant status to look for a cure for the boy) parsed the files, Danny raced his motorized chariot up and down and in and around the aisles between stacks, using a sawed-off hockey stick to whack a soccer ball, which he then chased, laughing.

Fortunately for all involved, the only other person using that lowest floor of the twelve-story stacks, deep inside the mammoth building and the cliff into which it was built, was an undergraduate blasting 50 Cent over headphones.

After Daniel's nearly two hours of soccer, minus occasional breaks for snacks and reading, Donovan was fed up and ready to put aside his research. Patrick McGowan truly had disappeared without the customary trace, at least so far as the files of the university where he made his name were concerned. He'd taken his true genius and amazing insights and blown town.

Which hardly meant that Donovan had given up the hunt. That had only begun.

He turned off his laptop, closed the lid, stretched, and yawned.

Danny breezed down along one stack—the one holding old doctoral theses from the chemistry department, Donovan thought—and turned, then made a sharp turn into the main aisle and past the three elevators. Few and far between, Donovan thought, were the libraries big enough to require three elevators to go from floor to floor.

Donovan imagined the squealing of tires as the boy aced the hairpin at Le Mans.

Danny kept twisting and angling to keep the ball out in front of "the Beast," as his new motorized chair was known. When he reached Donovan's cubicle, Danny shot the ball at his dad's feet, laughing. Donovan lifted them at the last moment, and, as the chair sped by in pursuit, called out, "Who's winning, Manchester United or Liverpool?"

It was a routine the father and son had.

"Liv-*pooool*," Danny shouted back.

"They had bloody well better," Donovan replied, using the patently phony brogue he used from time to time to amuse his son and himself.

When the chase had chased off back to the far end of the floor, silence fell from the sky. Donovan put the laptop in its case and zipped it up. He hefted the substantial black case, and then dropped it back to the floor. He muttered to the air, "When they told us that one day we'd all be using computers, they said nothing about carrying them around on our backs."

He leaned back and closed his eyes and wondered again where Patrick McGowan had gotten himself. Probably coaching for Aberdeen.

It was then that he heard the noise. The noises. Banging, or thumping. Scratching. Thumping *and* scratching. Coming from somewhere close by. Not from the stacks, though, but Donovan looked around to see nonetheless.

The scratching was like that made by a corpse trying to claw its way out of the coffin, not that Donovan could recall ever hearing that exact sound. The thumping was that of the side of a fist against iron. Donovan got to his feet.

The north wall of the basement library was concrete—made of blocks painted and painted again dozens of times, white now stained with rust. The wall was bare, nothing stood against it, save for an occasional stand-alone stack filled, like every other flat surface, with books or *something* that bore words.

The sound seemed to come from behind one of them. Donovan walked up to it. A yellowing old tag pronounced it an ar-

11

chive of dissertations presented to the physics faculty during the years 1952 to 1957.

The shelf did a proud job of hiding what was behind it—a rusting iron door, well under six feet high—that seemed tough enough to have held back the Johnstown Flood, and battered enough to have done so.

From behind that door came another couple of scratches, another knock.

"Hello?" Donovan asked.

Nothing. Silence on the other side. Someone listening? Donovan wondered.

"Anyone in there?" he asked, louder.

The answer was a flurry of knocks, decreasingly loud, decreasingly rapid, and at last the fading cry, "*Ayuda!*"

"*Ya voy,*" he replied.

Donovan muttered, "My apologies to the physics faculty," grabbing the shelf and yanking it away from the wall and door. Then he jumped out of the way as maybe a hundred forgotten dissertations, written by bright-eyed aspirants currently boring freshman at community colleges across the land, suffered another indignity.

The metal shelf clattered atop the dissertations, the sound echoing around the stacks.

That seemed to halt the soccer match. For shortly, the ball rolled by slowly, absent the sound of mechanized pursuit. Instead, Danny rolled to a stop next to the pile of papers.

"Whatcha doing, Daddy?" the boy asked.

"Making a mess."

"Is someone going to be mad at you?"

"Someone usually is," the Captain replied.

"Why'd you do that?" Danny asked.

"There's someone behind that door. Trapped behind that door."

"Why?"

"I heard something, like someone trying to get out. And he asked for help in Spanish. I told him I was coming."

"Open the door."

"Good idea," Donovan said, grabbing the iron latch, turning and yanking. The latch turned but the door didn't budge.

"Open it, Dad."

"I'm trying, boss. You want to give me a hand?"

"Okay!" the boy said, sunshine in his bright eyes.

"You pull on my belt, and I'll pull on the door."

The boy proudly grabbed hold of the back of his father's belt and pulled.

Donovan pulled on the door, hard, over and over, bracing his foot against the wall, pulling rhythmically. Then he kicked the base of the door. That seemed to do something, for the iron hinges creaked and some rust flaked off.

"That's it!" Danny said.

Donovan pulled with all his might, and slowly, as if reluctant to reveal the trouble hiding on the other side, the door creaked open. Donovan moved a mound of dissertations to one side with his foot and pulled the door as far open as it would go.

Danny let go of the belt.

Donovan saw a man, or the body of a man . . . he couldn't be sure which, given the darkness of a tunnel that went far beyond the reach of the light of the library. The man had dark complexion and hair, was twenty or so, and wore a Riverside University groundskeeper's uniform. He was lying on his side, curled in not quite a fetal position, so as better to scratch and claw at the door. A trail of blood led off into the dark.

Donovan's brain raced, at least to the extent it could after having scrutinized so much scientific material. He didn't think, *What if this poor bastard is dead?* He had seen so many bodies over the decades that he had become hard as rock on the matter. He thought, *How will I explain this to Danny?* who asked, "Who's that, Dad?"

Trying to think of something to say, he said, "I don't know."

"Is he sleeping?"

Donovan didn't reply, but crouched near the man's head and felt for a carotid pulse. He wasn't sure if he felt one . . . very faint, perhaps, but the skin was warm and then, suddenly, a groan and a twitch.

Donovan pulled his hand back.

"You woke him up," Danny said.

Whoever he was, the man tried to lift his head, flicking his eyes open and staring at the Captain in joy and fear.

He said one word, "mercury," and died, his head falling fully back down on the concrete.

"He went back to sleep," Danny said.

No longer was there a carotid pulse, no longer even the suggestion of one.

Oh balls, Donovan thought. His famous ability to run his mouth didn't account for the sometimes inability to run his brain. He did a silent sort of mental shrug to himself, grumbled, and got to his feet.

"There's something I have to talk to you about," he said to his young son. "But first I have to call Uncle Brian."

2. "WHEN MOST GUYS TAKE THEIR KIDS TO THE LIBRARY IT HAS SOMETHING TO DO WITH DR. SEUSS, NOT DR. DOOM"

"When most guys take their kids to the library it has something to do with Dr. Seuss," said Lieutenant Brian Moskowitz. "But with you, it's Dr. Doom."

"I didn't plan it this way," Donovan replied to his former subordinate, and still close friend, who had replaced him as chief of the NYPD's Department of Special Investigations.

Mosko continued, "It's kind of traditional to find something like *Sunshine, the Happy-Go-Lucky Sea Otter,* not *The Corpse in the Cave.*"

Donovan treated Mosko to the same gesture that went in the other direction for years.

The Captain said, "Danny and I were down here trying to track down a scientist who might be able to help with the paralysis."

"Did you find him?"

"Not yet. I don't even have a lead. He had a brilliant career going on here and then disappeared without a trace," Donovan said.

"Kind of like you, right?" Mosko smiled evilly, and for his efforts got himself another digital salute.

"I retired from the force to find someone who can help Danny. And also because it was the only way that *you* would be able to get anywhere in life."

Mosko offered his "you're full of shit" look.

"Other than by taking up a career as a personal trainer or

15

standup comic. Possibly both." Donovan returned the evil smile, and continued, doing Henny Youngman, saying, "Hey kid. Take my abs. Please."

Perhaps sensing that a change of topic would help, Mosko asked, "Where's Watson?"

"The second period has begun," Donovan replied, hooking a thumb down the floor to where the soccer game appeared to have begun again.

"Where did you tell him that people go when they die?"

"I said, 'You got a choice between heaven and Brooklyn,' " the Captain replied.

"No, what did you say?"

"I told him that he went to heaven to be with his mommy and daddy."

"What? What did you just tell me? You're a fucking atheist."

Donovan said, "It's a story that's worked for thousands of years. Who am I to argue with thousands of years of effective lying? Besides, Danny needs to know that his mommy and daddy will be with him always and that sounded like the best way to put it."

"Did he buy it?"

"Probably not," Donovan said.

Mosko sighed, looked around at the busy stacks of the library and the sad aloneness of the tunnel, and said, "Maybe your Patrick McGowan went in the tunnel looking for something and got himself lost and locked in," Mosko said. "Maybe that's him in the tunnel there."

He cocked his head in the direction of the body, which was being pored over by forensics genius Howard Bonaci and his crew of high-tech sleuths.

Donovan said, "Nice suggestion, were it not for the fact that McGowan was fifty-four when he disappeared. That would make him seventy-four or something now."

"Plastic surgery can do wonders. Look at Cher."

"McGowan was Irish. This guy is Latino."

"I was pulling your chain, Bill," Mosko said.

"Any idea who he is?" Donovan asked.

Mosko shook his head. "There's no ID on him. Not a damn thing. But he's lying on top of his wallet, so we don't want to move him until Howard's through."

"He's wearing a university work shirt," Donovan said.

"Roger that. I'm trying to get hold of the security chief at this place. By the way, I'm pretty sure you know him. He's another old Westie thug like you."

Mosko referred to the West Side Irish mob from the 1960s that, it was said, even the mafia feared. Donovan knew a couple of them; no one in his current life was sure how well, and he was intentionally circumspect on the matter.

"What's his name?" Donovan asked suspiciously.

"Thomas J. Keogh."

"The saints preserve us," Donovan said, crossing himself.

"Yeah, I kinda thought so. Tell me, when your black Jewish wife agreed to your retiring—"

"*Agreed?*"

"Did she have any idea she was throwing you back in with your old friends?"

"She's too busy being a lawyer to notice," Donovan said.

Mosko said, "Anyway, the vic died from three or four really serious blunt-instrument blows to the back of the head. There's a blood trail leading off into the tunnel."

"To where?" Donovan asked.

"We can't tell *that* until Forensics is finished with the body. We don't want to mess up evidence on this end before following the blood trail. Didn't you used to be a cop?"

"I was just thinking . . ."

"It's too cramped in the tunnel to walk around the body

17

without stomping evidence," Mosko said.

"Do we have any idea where the tunnel goes?" Donovan asked.

"What did you say?" Mosko asked.

"I asked where the tunnel goes," Donovan said.

"No, you asked if *we* know where the tunnel goes."

"So?"

"Who's this *we* you're talking about?" Mosko asked.

Donovan cleared his throat, shuffled his feet, and said, "Well, I can't seem to find Patrick McGowan for the moment, I have a little time on my hands, and—"

"Bill, can I be chief of the unit for five minutes before—?"

"You had five minutes. You caught the guy who was slaughtering the night shift at Bronx Terminal Market. In your first at-bat, you bagged a serial killer. You had *seven* minutes."

Mosko growled, the noise coming up from his fifty-inch chest and reverberating in his throat.

"I can *help*, maybe," Donovan said. "Danny and I can help."

Mosko held up a hand like a traffic cop in days of yore, and said, "Whoa! Wait! Time out! Fins!" He switched and began making a "time out" sign, chopping the side of one hand into the palm of the other.

At that moment, a soccer ball bounced off Mosko's legs, the legs accustomed to decades of jeans now startlingly clad in well-pressed gray wool slacks worn over Florsheim shoes. The Beast rolled up and came to a halt alongside Donovan and Mosko.

"Hi, Uncle Brian!"

Looking down and grinning, Mosko said, "Hiya, Chief. Who's winning, Manchester United or Liverpool?"

"Liv . . . *poool*," the boy said, using the hockey stick to start the ball rolling again. As he started after it, Donovan called out, "Uncle Brian says we can help him catch the person who hurt that man."

Danny made a whooping sort of noise, then, as he drove off, said, "Thanks, Uncle Brian." Who looked at his old boss and said, "I hate you more than fuckin' ever."

Donovan grinned.

3. DRINKING COFFEE AND STARING AT THE CASHIER'S ASS

Thomas J. Keogh was a retired cop like Donovan, but one of a wholly different stripe. As a member of the force he never rose above the rank of sergeant, mostly in the Bronx, and never got out of a uniform that over the years increasingly stretched at the belt and butt. He "put in his twenty" and retired at forty-something to go into private security, heading his one-man company. That meant, for the most part, that he drove around the rusty rundown warehouses and loading docks of his sole client, the Hunt's Point Cooperative Market in the Bronx in a Ford Crown Victoria—the vehicle most often associated with cops and cab drivers—that had a fancy sign on the door reading TJK Corporate Security.

Those who knew him were never quite sure what he *did* in the car beyond drink coffee and eat sticky buns picked up at one of the half-dozen 24/7/365 greasy spoons that vied with used car–part peddlers along Hunts Point Avenue. Therein lay a point of contention between Keogh and Moskowitz, for the NYPD Department of Special Investigations now headed by Mosko nabbed the serial killer of market workers, who Keogh barely knew was at work there. All Keogh knew is what all the rest of the City That Never Sleeps knew—that with alarming frequency a night-shift meat packer in his blood- and sweat-stained clothes would disappear on the long walk up Hunts Point Avenue in the dark, and the car parts, to be found later bludgeoned to death. When that murderer was safely behind bars and the problem of the Bronx district attorney, Mosko was given a good and sincere handshake by the commissioner as well as a "nice first at-bat" from the mayor, both of whom did a poor job of concealing their glee over Donovan being gone and having trained his successor so well. For if Donovan stopped being a loose cannon when he was made chief of the Department of Special Investigations, he retained his ability to get shot at. The latter happened now and again with bullets and once, nearly, with a crossbow bolt, but mostly with angry phone calls to city hall from tabloid and TV reporters he had insulted.

For years the brass wished Donovan well. For years they wished him gone, the mayor having gone so far at one point as to have bought him a reclining chair with the invitation to take things easy. When Donovan retired at the peak of his form and with his record intact, the brass felt certain that his exquisitely trained successor appeared to be much more of a team player.

Keogh wasn't quite so happy about the flow of events. When the news broke that the serial killer had been caught, he was sitting in a 24/7/365 bean wagon drinking coffee and staring at the cashier's ass. So while he never knew Mosko, Keogh knew that he wouldn't like him.

"Hey, Bill," he said, striding down the aisle in close pursuit of his beer belly, sticking his hand out.

"Good to see you, Tom," Donovan replied, grasping the outstretched hand and giving it a good pumping, but then pulling his hand back the better to hook a thumb in the direction of his successor. "Say hello to Brian."

Keogh said, "Hello."

Mosko said, "How ya doing, pal?" and then squeezed the man's hand hard enough to make the fingernails pop out.

It wasn't clear that Keogh got the message. But then, as Donovan oft demonstrated, the Irish are famously hard to read.

Donovan said, "It's been a long road from Hell's Kitchen.

You look good."

"You, too. I hear you got rich and retired."

"He got rich," Mosko said.

"I married a woman who is well-enough off to let me pursue other interests"—he paused as the other interest zipped by, waving and laughing—"and let me turn over the department to Brian."

"In a manner of speaking," Mosko said.

"I get to hang out with my old buddies again. I heard you had enough of the Bronx."

"Yeah," Keogh replied. And looking a bit cautiously, Donovan thought, at Mosko, added, "it was getting a little rough over there. Luckily, your successor made my life easier by taking one of the bad guys off the street. Funny how he did that. I never saw him around."

"Little red Corvette," Mosko said.

"Big white forensics van," Bonaci chimed in, getting to his feet and departing the vicinity of the corpse, leaving the latter to others to bag and bundle off. Almost immediately came the zip of a body bag.

He was introduced to Keogh, who appeared relieved that *somebody* could shake a hand gently.

"There's nothing but loading docks and trucks there," Keogh said. "And there are enough wise guys driving Corvettes."

Bonaci said, "Good to see you on the job again, Captain."

Growling, Mosko said, "He's not on the job. He's on the shit list. And his name is 'Bill.' "

"Whatever. Do you guys want a report on the delicti of the corpus or not?"

"*We* do," Donovan said, with a mischievous grin.

Once again, Mosko growled.

"The vic suffered blunt force trauma to the back of his head. I don't get paid what a doctor gets paid, but I would guess it was a subdermal hematoma that killed him. That, and the bleeding. What do they call it on *CSI*?"

"Exsanguination," Donovan replied.

"What?" Keogh asked.

"He bled to death," Mosko answered.

"Regarding the trauma, there were several blows, each about seven or eight centimeters across."

Keogh's face took on the look of someone who just realized his head was deliberately being talked over.

"About three inches," Mosko told him, with a bit of glee.

"Which means a pretty substantial weapon," Bonaci continued. "How he could crawl anywhere I can't tell you. The guy must have had a skull as thick as the brick that hit it."

"Brick?" Mosko asked.

"I say 'brick' only because that's about the size of the wound. The end of a brick. But as far as I can tell at first glance, there's no residue in the wound of the sort you would expect from a brick. Of course, we got to wait for more extensive lab work than I can do in the van."

"Are you keeping up with the payments on that thing?" Donovan asked his successor.

Donovan was ignored.

"I'll have a report sometime tomorrow afternoon," Bonaci said.

"Any idea where this happened?" Mosko asked.

The crime-scene guru nodded and said, "A rough one. The vic was bleeding in a steadily decreasing rate, so I can guess from the ten or twelve feet we followed the blood trail down into the tunnel. He was probably hit a hundred or a hundred-fifty feet down."

"One hundred and *fifty*?" Mosko asked.

"That's some hike," Keogh said, apparently glad to get a comment in.

"There are long tunnels everywhere under this city," Donovan said. In fact, the first case that got Donovan wide attention was that of a killer who used the tunnels under Riverside Park to flee the scene of his killings.

"Under the campus?" Mosko asked.

Donovan and Mosko looked at Keogh in vain, hoping his earlier comment would be succeeded by a contribution.

The campus security officer coughed into his hand and said, haltingly, "Yeah, well, I heard they were pretty long."

The two detectives exchanged faint smiles.

"There's got to be a map," Mosko said.

Donovan agreed and, sweeping a hand around the shelves of knowledge and trivia that surrounded them, said, "They keep everything."

Thinking of the elusive Patrick McGowan, he added, "*Almost* everything."

"Why don't you go see if you can find a map," Mosko said to Keogh.

"And while you're at it," Bonaci said, "The vic's ID says Gregorio Paz, age twenty-one, living at 54113 Broadway."

"Know him?" Mosko asked Keogh. Then, answering his question as well as sparing the former officer further embarrassment, added, "Nah, of course you couldn't. This is a big place."

"Yeah, sure is," Keogh replied, smiling. Looking over at the body bag, which was on its way to one of the elevators on a gurney he said, "He's Spanish?"

"Latino," Donovan replied.

"Did he say anything to you?" Mosko asked.

"He said, '*Ayuda.*' "

"What's that mean?" Keogh asked.

"Help," Donovan replied.

"Knowing *him*," Mosko said, cocking his head in Donovan's direction, "It was '*Ayuda! Necesito una cerveza.*' "

"My beer-drinking days are over," Donovan snarled.

"Yeah, but you just now hit the old neighborhood. Don't touch that dial."

"You guys speak a lot of Spanish," Keogh said.

"What, when you were a cop nobody Latino ever asked you for help?" Mosko replied.

"In my day, the Spanish spoke English. They figured if they were gonna live here they ought to learn the language. Not any more."

"People are entitled to speak their own language," Donovan said.

Keogh grumbled, then said, "If they're gonna get jobs—"

"Hey, pal," Mosko interrupted. "They do the work 'Americans' "—he made quotation marks in the air with his fingers—"they do the work Americans don't want to do anymore."

"Like care about others," Donovan said under his breath.

"All I know is the ones I see don't speak English. I don't speak Spanish. So how come you know so much Spanish?"

"Tengo muchos amigos latinos," Donovan said to an increasingly flustered Keogh, who was just smart enough to realize he had better watch what he said on the subject of race from that point.

"Y un niño," Mosko added.

When Donovan gave him a dirty look, Mosko pretended not to notice, but said, "How about that map?"

"All right, I'll go look for one," Keogh said, clearly cheered at the prospect of getting away from the two of them.

"And Paz's personnel folder, please."

Keogh trudged off to the elevator, where he waited impatiently while Paz's body was loaded onto one of the cars and taken upstairs.

When the campus security chief was gone, Mosko laughed.

25

"Where did we get that *dinosaur?*"

"The bad old days of cop-dom, my friend, when certain cops were just born to be fat and lazy one day. Keogh just peaked early. Thanks for mentioning Lewis, by the way."

"Keogh doesn't *habla*. He bragged about it, didn't he? Besides, you're no longer on the force and you retired having made Pilcrow look good."

Deputy Chief Inspector Paul Pilcrow was Donovan's long-standing nemesis. He *hated* Donovan, mainly for being an opinionated loose cannon who nonetheless got things done, and often brilliantly. It would have been rough on young patrolman Lewis Rodriguez were Pilcrow to find out that he was the result of Donovan's long-ago relationship with a Cuban barmaid named Rosalie Rodriguez. But Donovan *had* made Pilcrow look good in the course of his part in the 9/11 investigation; so much so that the two parted company on as good terms as might be expected.

"I suppose," Donovan said.

"Where *is* Lewis these days?"

"Around. Working in the three-oh."

"Here?" Mosko asked, pointing at the floor.

"On Broadway," Donovan replied, pointing up. "He's on routine patrol. Other than that, he's chasing women and enjoying all three bedrooms in my old apartment."

"Probably all three at the same time."

"No doubt."

"So Paz said what to you, just *'ayuda'?*"

"That's it. 'Help.' Then when I—"

Daniel had rolled up. The soccer match having ended in a clear victory for Liverpool some time earlier, the boy had spent another hour in a study cubicle reading a book about cars.

Donovan continued, "Then when Daniel and I got the door open, Paz said one word—'mercury.' "

26

" 'Mercury?' That was it?"

Donovan nodded.

"Meaning what, the temperature?"

The Captain shrugged.

"I don't suppose he meant Freddie Mercury."

"Doubt it."

"What other mercuries are there?" Mosko asked.

"The planet," Donovan said. Then he added, "Or the mythological figure."

"Greek god of what, speed?"

"Yep. But he could have meant the toxic heavy metal."

"The same thing as the thermometer mercury," Mosko said.

"I'll Google the word when I get home and see how many other mercuries come up."

"I can do it now," Mosko said, pulling Donovan toward the spot where he had cleared off a shelf—old and yellowing doctoral dissertations were taking yet another beating at the hands of law enforcement—for his laptop and did some keystrokes.

"I hope they have broadband in here," he said.

"In a university library?"

Sure enough, Mosko soon was able to say, "Mercury poisoning. Some fish got it."

"And the Mad Hatter," Donovan replied. "They used to use it to make felt. It made them crazy."

"I thought that Chinese imports made them crazy."

"That, too."

"Mercury Sable," Daniel chimed in.

"Whazzat, boss?" Donovan asked.

"A car!" the boy said brightly.

Mosko added, "Upscale Ford Taurus. One or two grand extra for the right to claim you don't drive a Ford."

"Cars are *your* area, the two of you," Donovan said. "How

about Mercury Outboards?"

"How do you know something about outboard motors?" Mosko asked.

"Marcie spent a summer on a boat at the Seventy-ninth Street Boat Basin, remember?"

"A Latino guy dying in a tunnel in Manhattan bedrock won't have as his last words the name of a brand of outboard motor. What's he asking for, a Viking funeral? Put my body in a rowboat, set it on fire, and aim me at the middle of New York Harbor?"

"This is going nowhere," Donovan said.

"I'm going to go down the tunnel," Mosko said to his old boss and to Bonaci, who had wandered over with a look of completion on his face. "You're welcome to *come along.*"

Donovan smiled.

"Can I come too?" Daniel asked. In his eyes was that look of expectancy kids get as the Christmas presents are being opened.

"Howard, is that okay with you?" Mosko asked.

"Yeah, sure. You, the Captain, Watson, whomever." And to Daniel he added, "How you doin', guy?"

"Okay, Uncle Howard."

Mosko asked, "Are your guys done over there?"

"Mercury Morris," Bonaci replied.

"What?" Donovan asked.

"Football player. Running back. Miami. Early 1970s. Where were you, Captain?"

"At a Blarney Stone on Third Avenue working on his case of amnesia," Mosko said. "And his name really *is* 'Bill.' "

He slapped Donovan's shoulder.

Again the Captain smiled. "I heard the name. Thought he was a Giant, though. I guess I'm sports-impaired."

"And wasn't there a Mercurio in Shakespeare someplace?" Bonaci continued.

"Mercutio. *Romeo and Juliet.* He was stabbed to death, setting off a train of events."

"There you go," Mosko said. "He really said 'Mercutio' and you didn't hear him right because old guys have hearing problems."

Mosko got the finger again.

"What I'm wondering," Donovan said, "is why he called for help in Spanish and said his last word in English. On the other hand, 'mercury' in Spanish is *mercurio.*"

"I rest my case about your hearing," Mosko said.

"My father hears okay," Daniel said. "Every time I open a bag of potato chips he hears it."

"I don't think we're dealing with Shakespeare," Bonaci said. "Our vic was *beaten,* not stabbed."

"Minor difference. Anyway, 'mercury' means 'fast,' and our guy sure wasn't."

Mosko nodded in the direction of the tunnel, and added, "It must have taken him a long time to crawl down that tunnel. Got any idea from where?"

Bonaci nodded. "We found the place where he was attacked and where he crawled away from. We swept it for trace, took photos, picked some bits of paper and other junk, took measurements, the whole nine yards. Now it's up to you guys to figure out what happened."

"You're all done?"

"A few things left to do, so don't mess around too much," Bonaci said.

Then Bonaci touched Daniel's arm and asked, "Are you ready to tell these bums what the story is?"

"Let's go!" the boy said happily.

4. "THE REASON YOU'RE HERE, OTHER THAN TO FIND BODIES AND MAKE MY LIFE MISERABLE"

Donovan and son followed Mosko and Bonaci into the tunnel, which was six feet high, so both Donovan and Mosko had to duck down a bît. But it was a good fifteen feet wide, which left plenty of room for the Beast to fit in without squishing the already examined blood trail or other evidence.

The floor was flat concrete, but the walls were rough granite blocks. At first the floor was thick with the dust of ages, but as the search party made its slow progress, there appeared the mild sort of dusting found in basement storage areas that hadn't been visited in ten or fifteen years.

And there was a *lot* of storage. Both walls were lined with box upon box—sometimes three or four piled one on the other and crammed tightly against their neighbors. Some were marked only with penciled dates going back to the 1910s and 1920s. Others had typed labels held in place with adhesive tape now yellowed and crumbling.

At one point some unremembered academic obsessive-compulsive had tried to create order. The labels were uniform, bearing such basic information as "Dissertations, Chemistry, 1937" and "Student Records, Zoology, 1917." In more recent decades, the order had broken down and some boxes were unmarked. Most were cardboard, but a few were wooden and one or two were made of tin. Further, the labeling increasingly was raggedy, such as "Fac Recs, 1964" or "Postdocs, 1973."

Donovan eyeballed the boxes in the latter categories.

★ ★ ★ ★ ★

The hub that united the wagon wheel of tunnels was octagonal and, at about fifty feet in diameter, surprisingly large. Tunnel entrances, eight of them, perforated it in perfect symmetry.

"This is *big*," Mosko said.

"The university uses *it* for storage too."

"Why isn't there anything stored in it now?" Daniel asked. Mosko looked down on him and smiled.

"So why isn't there?" Mosko asked Keogh.

"Beats me."

"There's something special about this room," Donovan said, wandering over to a patch of brick and staring at it.

"Yeah, somebody got clubbed to death in it," Keogh said.

Yellow crime-scene tape surrounded a patch of concrete in the center of the room. There, technicians had marked off the scene of the attack. A large spray of blood extended away from the tunnel to the Franks Library, while a smaller fan of blood went at right angles to it. The blood trail began near the smaller fan, in a large blob that turned into a teardrop and then decreasingly large drops, some of which were smudged by Paz having dragged himself through them. By the time it reached the tunnel to Franks, the drops had stopped, leaving only a slowly dying trail.

"The floor is clean," Mosko said. "No dust. No dirt."

"No footprints," Bonaci said.

"Wiped clean?"

"Everywhere. Not under the blood, of course, but everywhere else. And what's under the blood looks mainly like a job for Mr. Clean. We'll know better after you guys have your look and get out of here."

"There's got to be *something*," Mosko said.

"Yeah, a floor that's been wiped clean in all directions."

"Oh, *balls*," Mosko said.

"This could be what I've been looking for," he said, more or less to himself.

"What?" Mosko asked, over his shoulder.

"Records, possibly concerning Patrick McGowan."

"Who? Oh, right. The reason you're here, other than to find bodies and make my life miserable."

"I've got to come back and go through these boxes," Donovan said.

"Why not do it now and leave me alone?"

"Lead on," Donovan said.

The tunnel was lit by a string of bare bulbs hung from the ceiling every ten or twenty feet. Some were very old, unfrosted ones that cast a yellow pall over the fading cardboard boxes near them. But here and there, forensic techs had set up portable lights.

Bonaci said, "We followed the blood trail down the tunnel, about a hundred and fifty feet to the east."

"We're going north, Uncle Howard," Daniel said.

"Okay, north. You're right. Thanks."

"It's okay," Daniel said, clearly proud of himself.

"The tunnel meets up with two others. There's a crossroads. I don't know where the others go."

"To other buildings," a voice said. It was Keogh, coming from up ahead, from the direction of the scene of the crime.

"Tom?" Mosko asked, a bit suspiciously.

Keogh appeared from the shadow in a stretch of tunnel where the ancient light bulbs had blown out and where no forensics lighting had been set up. But as he stepped to the center of the tunnel, it was backlit by the glow from the lights illuminating the murder scene.

"How'd you get there?" Mosko asked.

"I found the map. It was in the security office, in an old file drawer. I came in from the basement of the chapel."

"The chapel," Mosko said.

"Yeah. St. Andrew Avolino's. There's a door in the basement leading to the tunnels. I don't know what the priest uses it for."

"Catacombs, maybe," Donovan said.

"It looked like it hadn't been opened in years. I guess they don't get bodies all that often."

Donovan sensed that the man had grown more secure and comfortable, having scored a hit in relatively short order. Maybe he hadn't lost *all* his cop training.

"Did you step on anything?" Bonaci asked.

"Nah. I ran into one of your guys and he said you were done with collecting evidence. But I was careful anyway. Want to look at the map?"

Mosko said that they did, and Keogh laid it out atop a pile of boxes, the top one of which was labeled "Zoology Specimens 1947–1949."

The map was a fourteen-by-seventeen copy of the original or something like it. At some point someone had block printed "CAMPUS TUNNELS/STORAGE 1968." It showed a spider web of tunnels radiating out from a central hub, resembling somewhat the roads leading to the Arc de Triomphe in Paris. Each tunnel ended in a building, presumably in the basements.

"Where are we now?" Mosko asked.

"Halfway between Franks and the Arc de Triomphe," Keogh said. He pronounced it like "try oomph," as if that were an energy drink. He seemed proud that, having flunked Spanish, he was try-oomphing in French.

"We just call it 'the Hub,' " Keogh said.

Mosko said, "And you call the library Franks? After what? Nathan's?" Mosko asked.

"Brooklyn again," Donovan muttered.

"After some old guy who worked here. A scientist. Won the Nobel Prize, I think."

Donovan said, "Samuel Franks is professor emeritus of physics. He won the Nobel for his work on the Manhattan Project."

"The bomb," Mosko said.

"The bomb."

"They gave out a Nobel Prize for working on the atomic bomb?" Mosko asked.

"Alfred Nobel invented dynamite," Donovan replied.

"Some of the stuff was done in the basement—well, the second sub-basement—of the physics building," Keogh said. "It's a national historical site or something like that."

"Franks has got to be in his nineties now," Donovan said.

Keogh nodded. "You'll see him around. He kind of wanders around smiling and asking how things work. A couple of years ago we installed security stations that look like high-tech phone booths. One day I was driving the perimeter and saw Franks poking his head into one of them and pestering my guard to explain how the intercom system works. He won a Nobel Prize and now has to know how the intercom works. The old guy's into everything. A lot of people say he's lost it."

"Samuel Franks has lost it like more than ninety-nine percent of the people on the globe ever had it," Donovan said.

"I don't know," Keogh said. "He's got a keeper."

"A what?" Mosko asked.

"A nurse, you know. She follows him around. Keeps him on a short leash."

"Does he have medical problems?" Donovan asked.

"Franks is *ninety.*"

"So's my mother, and she just stopped doing her own carpentry five or six years ago."

Clearly eager to get back on topic, Mosko asked, "So where was the body found—on the map, I mean? Point it out for me."

Keogh tapped a meaty finger on the Hub.

"There's footprints in all the tunnels, maybe too many to catalog. We'll get on that, too. I gotta tell you this, though. This is the cleanest crime scene I've ever seen."

"Even the walls," Donovan said, waving them over to where he stood peering at the bricks.

He ran a fingertip along the top of one, along the slight projection, like an admiral doing his white-glove inspection of the boiler room. Barely a trace of dust stuck to his fingertip. "Whoever did this did it pretty well," he said.

Daniel drove the Beast over, looked at the brick, and said, "This is cleaner than your shop, Dad."

Mosko laughed.

Keogh asked, "The cleaning lady isn't allowed in the basement?"

"My basement is sacred, a man's sanctum, like it should be, the repository of tools, CD players, beer, and dirty socks. Brian—you know *him*, the guy who inherited my old job—and I had this discussion last Christmas. You like this room, Daniel?"

The boy said, "Yeah. I could play a great game of dodgeball down here."

"When was the last time something was stored down here?" Mosko asked.

"I'll see if I can find out," Keogh replied, then disappeared down one of the tunnels.

"What's east of here?" Mosko asked no one in particular, while nodding in the direction of Keogh's disappearing footsteps.

"That's west," Daniel said.

"Thanks," Mosko said.

"This makes no sense," Donovan said.

"No shit." Then Mosko looked down at the boy, shrugged, and added, "Being around *you* I don't have to apologize for my language."

"He's a city kid."

Daniel smiled.

"There's crap stored in all the tunnels, right?" Donovan asked.

"Right," Bonaci called from across the room, where he was bent over watching as a forensics tech shined a colored light of some sort on the floor at the entrance to a tunnel that went, Daniel didn't get the chance to say, to the northwest.

"Why not here?"

"Maybe they were getting ready for something. You know, cleaning up."

"What?" Donovan asked.

He strolled back to the wall and stuck a finger in one of the inch-wide, threaded lead pipes that punctuated the wall like rivets, at about knee level and three feet apart.

"We need Howard to take a closer look to see what these pipes were used for," Donovan said. Then, catching himself and smiling at his former apprentice, added, "That *you* need to find out about."

"Thank you," Mosko said, with gentility that was a bit forced, coming from someone from Canarsie.

Followed by his son, Donovan peered down each of the tunnels in turn, at one point using his Maglite to look over the shoulder of a forensics tech. There were boxes in each tunnel, the same sort of storage crates that Donovan found in the first one.

"This is just the same as the tunnel that Daniel and I found. So why are things stored everywhere but here?"

"I tried lifting a couple of 'em," Bonaci said. "They're *heavy*. You ever try lifting a box full of paper?"

Donovan had, and not so long ago, and he said so. "Yeah. The boxes containing the records I was going through trying to track down Patrick McGowan."

Then Donovan yawned, stretched arms that were, in fact, still smarting from having done so. Then he said, "This is thrilling, but as much as I would like to hang around and tilt at windmills with you, I have this sudden urge for pizza."

"Yeah!" Daniel said.

Mosko seemed surprised but happy. He said, "You're a wise man."

"With pepperoni," Daniel said.

"I seem to recall a nice greasy pizza joint up on Broadway a few blocks downtown."

"Let's go!"

5. WHEN NORMALLY SANE PEOPLE DUG GOPHER HOLES BENEATH THE CRUST OF THE EARTH

The following day, Donovan found himself patronizing Starbucks, an act he performed with a certain reluctance.

Starbucks made fine coffee and Donovan liked it. He would drink more of it were it not for the association with nouveaux riche, which technically speaking Donovan was, although he would sooner have his flesh ripped by demons than admit it.

There was a Starbucks every seven to ten blocks all the way up Broadway from Wall Street to Columbia University at, or about, the junction of 116th Street. When there wasn't an actual Starbucks within clear sight of a pedestrian, there was one of the many Starbucks imitators. They too were good, but the whole pricey coffee thing left Donovan wondering if it shouldn't be called "Joe" but "Joseph." *Sir* Joseph. He preferred his coffee to be what he called "basic bodega." That is to say, "coffee, milk, two sugars," served in one of those iconic New York City paper coffee cups printed with drawings of amphora and Greek columns. And printed with the words "We are happy to serve you," which have been kicking around since the mid-sixties when someone decided that only Greeks sold coffee.

He kept one of those cups and the now-cold coffee inside it a safe distance away from the yellowing folder before him. Donovan was back at the same study desk as the day before, the difference being the absence of a body. A cardboard box of similar folders sat on the floor nearby. Not quite too near was the entrance to the tunnel in which Daniel and he found Paz the

38

day before. It was still roped off. A solitary forensic tech loitered there, probing the walls with an instrument that looked like a notebook computer wired to a dill pickle. Donovan was disinterested in the details of high-tech probing of bricks. He had things to do while Daniel was at school.

The Captain ran a finger down a page of notes, jottings made in an odd, random combination of script and block letters. Words sprang off the page—tremor (crossed out, and rather violently); dysautonomia (crossed out); gait (dimple); wheelchair (dimple); bradykinesia (crossed out); blepharospasm (crossed out); lead pipe rigidity (two dimples!); and cog-wheeling (crossed out twice). Finally, the entire passage was crossed out. There also were deep dimples in the paper where someone, presumably McGowan, stabbed it with an angry ballpoint pen. Black ink.

Not only had McGowan stabbed his own notes, he seemed to have done so with a pattern and a purpose. Donovan stared at the words for several minutes, trying combinations of the dimpled words—gait, wheelchair, lead pipe rigidity. Getting nowhere on his own, he turned to his laptop, went online, and keyed in the words. After a very short time he signed out, and shut off the laptop.

"Parkinson's," he muttered. "Wrong disease."

Frustrated and a little bored, Donovan stashed the machine in his old leather shoulder bag. After a few pleasantries with the tech who was wielding what the Captain thought of as "the electric pickle," he squeezed past the man and strolled down the tunnel.

The storage boxes had been gone through by Bonaci's crew and put back in not quite the same spots. Donovan took out his Maglite and did some poking of his own.

Nothing much came to his eye at first. There were doctoral dissertations one upon the other, enough to make him wonder if there weren't in America more PhDs than pizza deliverymen. There also were more mundane records, paperwork, and, closest to the Hub, a cluster of boxes from the early 1960s. Among them was a boxful of yellowing, and at the edges, crumbling, copies of the college's student newspaper.

There were a dozen copies of one dated November 8, 1962. They were neatly bound by a thin rubber band that snapped in two at his touch. He picked up one and scanned the front page. Below an account of the campus response to the Cuban Missile Crisis was a pro-and-con about the wisdom of fallout shelters.

The nuclear holocaust panic of fall and winter 1962 was at the dawn of the Captain's consciousness. He was barely Daniel's age when normally sane people dug gopher holes beneath the crust of the Earth and lined them with concrete, there to ride out the expected white flash of nuclear blast and consequent fallout.

"Fallout," Donovan mused. In the twenty-first century that referred mainly to hair. Thankfully, that meant only a fraction of his hair. He remained far ahead of Moskowitz in the keeping-one's-hair department, so much so that the latter bought a tee shirt reading, "Real men don't waste hormones growing hair."

Then Donovan's eyebrows sought the ceiling. The author of the paper opposing fallout shelters for being useless, pointless, and Pollyannish was Richard Marlowe, Donovan's old Broadway bar friend. He was the one who daily aced the *New York Times* crossword puzzle, once or twice in under ten minutes. (The Captain's best time was twenty-three minutes, and, amidst word competition with Marlowe, he often gave up and returned to his bottle of Pabst Blue Ribbon beer.)

Marlowe liked talking about the Cuban Missile Crisis, especially how he organized an end-of-the-world beer party on the cliff overlooking the Hudson River. That was the cliff into which was built the Franks Library. He and ten or fifteen like-minded junior faculty and PhD candidates joined the usual suspects from Broadway to drink Knickerbocker beer—by the twenty-first century as long gone as fallout shelters—and wait for the fireball that they figured would hit Wall Street and race up Broadway faster than a talent agent in hot pursuit of his ten percent.

Donovan hadn't seen Marlowe in seven or eight years and wondered if he was still alive. The last Donovan heard, the man had retired on the modest pension given an associate professor of English. "Maybe I'll go up to Broadway and see if the sonofabitch is still alive," Donovan muttered to himself. "Maybe I'll see if he can still do the *Times* crossword puzzle in under ten minutes."

But first he had to finish his perusal of the storage boxes. That one box had more of the same—more stacks of stuff devoted to the nuclear terror of the early 1960s in general and the Cuban Missile Crisis in particular. Of that, Donovan had read enough to be able to brief those too young to appreciate how nuclear dread made everyone almost crazy in the years before Vietnam *made* everyone crazy. And how that dread was capsulized the night when a Russian ship carrying potentially nuclear-tipped missiles to Cuba approached the picket line of American warships blockading the same.

Blam! The end of the future! An array of things would never touch down on Earth. No Nixon presidency. No Beatles. No Kennedy or King assassinations. No *Star Trek*. No disco or punk rock. No personal computers, cell phones, or iPods. No Oprah, Dr. Phil, Paris Hilton, or *Da Vinci Code*.

Donovan mused, *Upon further thought . . .*

Turned to vapor the Knickerbocker beer would be, and with it the revelers using it to wash down, appropriately, their Cuban sandwiches.

Somehow that didn't happen. Soviet Premier Khrushchev

blinked, and the party raged on 'til dawn and universal hangovers embraced universal relief. Peace reigned on the strip of grass and concrete that separated the uptown and downtown lanes of Broadway.

Donovan resealed the box and left it among the several others that recorded the feat of those times. Curious, he thought, the boxes quite recently had been moved, slid along the floor from the direction of the Hub, something that Bonaci's crew wouldn't do, thus presumably occurring before the crime. Frayed edges on the leading edges of the boxes at the bottom of the piles told *that* story.

Probably meaningless, Donovan thought, and strolled back down the tunnel to the library, then took the elevator up and out of the building.

It was a fine spring afternoon, crisp and scented with a saltwater breeze drifting up the hill from the Hudson River, up the side streets and between the campus buildings. It was still a bit cold for shorts and tee shirts, and the grass of the quad had no Frisbee slingers. Donovan wasn't sure if anyone played Frisbee anymore, and certainly no one did it with the flair that he did in Riverside Park with Rosalie Rodriguez, his long-ago Cuban barmaid lover and the mother of Lewis, Donovan's first son. Some times those were.

Light jackets and notebook computers sprouted like crocuses on the immense rectangle of grass, hedges, and red brick paths, overall the size of six square blocks, that stretched from the Franks Library to the administration building and its oft-photographed clock tower.

The latter seemed to appear in the background every time a TV reporter brought a microphone to his lips and waxed wise on topics such as financing for higher education, the paucity of women PhDs in math and the sciences, or the latest casualties of binge drinking.

The clock rang four. "The sun is over the yardarm," Donovan thought as he walked toward Broadway and the bar.

As he passed the center of the quad, he paused before the bronze statue of Martin Luther King Jr. It was marked with the legendary civil rights leader's birth date, the date of his assassination, and the words "I have a dream."

Something bothered the Captain about that statue. He had no idea what. Maybe there should be a longer quote, he mused. Then he discarded the idea and continued on his way across and out of the campus.

At the brink of Broadway he paused a second time to turn and look back at the statue. Then he took out his camera phone, snapped a picture of the scene, and called his son's nanny. School was out and he had grown lonely.

The Rosa Blanca stood midway in a block on the uptown side of Broadway, next door to a *cambiamos cheques* joint where those without benefit of birth certificate or bank account could walk in, cash a paycheck, buy a phone card, and wire money home to the family in Paraguay. On the other side was a bodega selling *carnes y parrilladas* as well as rice on which to serve your meats and barbeque sauces. Both shops were done in Caribbean primary colors—bright yellows, blues, and orange. In other words, it was difficult to mistake one for a Crabtree & Evelyn outlet.

Each of the shop windows were plastered with hand-lettered signs in Spanish, so many that it was nearly impossible to see inside.

The Rosa Blanca was more conventional. Apart from the expected neon signs advertising Corona and Bud Light, there was one large sign, like its neighbors hand-lettered but on shirt cardboard, a child's scrawl that to Donovan seemed vaguely familiar.

CERVEZA FRIA.

He went inside.

And came right back out.

"It's a fucking nightmare," he said to the No Parking sign, which politely declined to respond.

6. HOOSIER DADDY

Then he thought again, took a deep breath, and surveyed the city scene before him. It came to him, and in a heartbeat. He was home.

Upper Broadway as it cut through West Harlem was no upper-middle-class outpost. The storm of strivers unleashed on Manhattan during the Giuliani years had yet to *entirely* drown the inner city. Real people with blue collars and white collars and no collars, who worked and sweated squeaked by supporting large families on the minimum wage, or nearly so. They walked past him with shopping carts and kids and dogs, and came out of the bodega with *pañales* to put on babies' bottoms. They went into the *cambiamos cheques* to wire a couple of bucks home to Paraguay, and because there was no money left, they were judicious about going into the Rosa Blanca for *cerveza, fria* or otherwise.

They were not at all like those in the world of One Police Plaza or Greenwich Village townhouses, Starbucks or Whole Foods, or the pricey sidewalk cafés of downtown where one could get a burrito for twenty bucks and say *gracias* condescendingly to the Mexican busboy.

"It's not a fucking nightmare," Donovan said, and this time he felt that the No Parking sign was beginning to understand. "It's fucking providence. I'm home."

He turned to go back into the bar, and as he turned he noticed that, unlike the stores on either side, it had never been a routine retail outlet. It had once been a gas station or auto repair shop or, going back far enough, a place to polish the horse-drawn buggy. A huge Roman arch of red brick, bleached by decades of blinding afternoon sun, soared over what once was a garage entrance big enough for at least one car and maybe two buggies. The entrance was long since bricked up, and now contained only the smoky and fly-specked window lit by beer signs that was cut into it.

Donovan smiled. While this wasn't precisely the old neighborhood he knew as little more than a lad, who had just joined the police force and was beginning to make a name for himself when he wasn't drinking himself into a stupor—that was forty or fifty blocks downtown and now littered with Starbucks coffee cups that stank of caramel mocha latte—it was close enough.

He went inside.

While ten or twenty men and women were at the bar, two familiar faces stood out nearest the door, one standing behind the bar and the other seated in front of it. The latter looked up, waggled the fingers of one hand, and smiled, before returning to his crossword puzzle.

The other one, in quick sequence, scowled and grinned evilly. "You had the right idea a minute ago," George Kohler said. "Get the fuck outta my bar."

George was as beer-bellied and bearded as a quarter century before, but gravity and age had done their work. His hair was pure white and the belly now sagged lumpily over the leather weight belt that struggled to support it. The Tin Lizzie was in need of a new engine.

Donovan reached across the bar and shook his hand. "The last time I saw you, other than on the wall at the post office, you were mixing apple martinis at the place around the corner from me. What's that place called? Oh, 'Emerald I'll.' Clever. Apple martinis."

It was in the suddenly trendy, historic Gansevoort Meat Market slice of the West Village. It was the sort of saloon that served up expensive drinks to real and wannabe actors, actresses, and not-quite-shaven celebrity bloggers. It was the sort of saloon often cited in the "seen at" sections of *Vanity Fair* and *GQ*.

"I got my ass the hell out of there," George snarled. "I hate you people."

"Excuse me?" Donovan replied.

"You rich guys and your posh neighbors are the ones who drove apartment rentals into the stratosphere."

Marlowe smiled, then swiveled around, took the Captain's hand, and said, "How are you, William?"

"Good. Getting better. What did this fuck just call me?"

He tilted his head in the direction of the bartender.

"He's *rich!*" George said to Marlowe, as if addressing Donovan directly might put him in danger of something contagious.

"My *wife* is rich," Donovan replied.

"Oh. Forgive me. Didn't she buy you a *townhouse?*"

"It was in the family," Donovan said, starting to get annoyed at being under assault for the financial good fortune that gave him the wherewithal to retire from finding murderers so he could concentrate on finding a cure for his son.

Turning to Marlowe, he asked, "Are you still doing the puzzle in under ten minutes?"

The man shook his head a bit and pouted slightly. "I just don't have it anymore. The arthritis"—he squeezed the fingers of one hand with the other hand—"has ended my ability to sprint. The best I can do is twelve minutes."

"*He* can't do much anymore, either," George said, tilting his head toward Donovan.

Marlowe tapped a finger on the puzzle before him. "Puns and word plays. Maybe you can help. You were always good

47

at funny stuff."

"Like imagining him no longer walking on his knuckles," Donovan said, tilting *his* head toward the bartender.

George scoffed and took a sip of draft beer. He always had one within reach, going back a quarter century. It was kind of a totem that was ever in sight, like the Tlingit Indian totem poles meant to assure a good salmon harvest.

Marlowe said, "Twelve letters. The second letter is 'o' and the last letter is 'y.' And the clue is 'Indianapolis roué's query.' "

" 'Indianapolis roué's query,' " George echoed, imitating Ed McMahon.

"The best minds of this bar are stumped," Marlowe said.

"Both of 'em," George added.

"Two men," Donovan replied. "One mind."

He leaned forward and peered at the puzzle, pausing a second to scratch the bridge of his nose. Then he straightened up and said, " 'Hoosier daddy'? Can I have a bottle of Bud?"

Marlowe groaned, put his head down on the bar, then his shoulders, and shook with chuckles.

"What did you say?" George asked.

"Hoosier daddy," Donovan replied, spelling it out this time.

"No. After that."

"I said I wanted a bottle of Bud," Donovan replied.

Marlowe lifted his forehead from the bar and aimed it at Donovan. "You're drinking?" he asked.

"Well, apparently I'm *not*," the Captain replied.

"Lemme get this straight," George said. "You want a bottle of Bud?"

"No. I want to wire ten bucks to Paraguay. I must have walked in the wrong door."

He began to make motions toward it.

"You fell off the wagon?" George asked.

"I suppose you could say that. I suppose the reason you didn't hear the thud is that it happened in New Orleans."

"New Orleans," Marlowe said flatly.

"You know a better place for it?"

"When in New Orleans?" George asked.

"A month or two ago," Donovan said.

"What were you doing there?" Marlowe asked.

Donovan said, "Looking for someone."

"If it was Fats Domino he got washed away," George said. "His piano, too. 'Blueberry Hill' wasn't high enough."

"It was a scientist named Patrick McGowan. I heard he was at Tulane for a while. He used to toil in the same vineyard as you."

"Riverside?"

"Yeah. Did you know him?" Donovan asked.

"I didn't know anyone in the sciences."

"I thought I was closing in on him and that a clue to his whereabouts might be in Tulane's faculty records, but unfortunately . . ."

"They kept them in the basement," Marlowe said.

"And some undergrounds are dryer than others," Donovan said, thinking of the tunnels across the street. "By the time I got there, they were in Baton Rouge and looked like spackle."

"Who'd this guy kill?" George asked.

"No one, and I'm not in that line of work anymore. He's someone who might be able to help Danny."

Because it had been a while, Donovan had to bring Marlowe up to date about Danny and his paralysis.

"So anyway, there I was in New Orleans and the trail had— pardon the expression—dried up, once again I couldn't help my son, and I was in the only city in the world other than New York that I could ever live in, and it was nearly annihilated, and I figured what the fuck? I went into that place on Bourbon Street down east, away from the honky-tonk part, that stayed open all through the hurricane, through every damn minute, they just drank their way through the whole thing. Six or seven days had passed and those guys were still in there, so I had a beer with them. Moreover, I bought the bar a round. I'm *rich*, remember? Call FEMA and report me."

"Do you want bottle or tap?" George asked, reaching for the former.

"Bottle."

"Do you want to talk about this?" Marlowe asked.

"Talk about what?"

Donovan accepted the bottle and took a sip.

"About *what?*" Marlowe said, crossing himself despite being an Episcopalian. "About why you're drinking again after, what, ten years?"

"Fifteen. When did *you* enroll in the Substance Abuse Storm Troopers? Sitting there with your bottle of Michelob every day for how many years?"

"Thirty or forty. I just turned seventy, so maybe it's more like fifty."

"The bars may change but the boozing goes on," Donovan said.

"I'm not addicted," Marlowe said. "I can stop any time I want."

"How about tomorrow?"

"I'm not ready. Ask me again when I'm eighty."

Donovan continued, "Okay, so in New Orleans I had a bottle of beer. Turbodog, if you must know."

"Turbodog?" Marlowe asked.

"A local dark ale. I had another beer—Blue Point Ale—two weeks ago at Brian Moskowitz's birthday party. And this one. Three beers in a month, and you assholes won't stop asking me dumbass questions so I can enjoy one of 'em."

He tapped the bottle with a fingertip.

George said, "I thought that staying on the wagon was a condition of your keeping the Captain's badge."

"It is. Was. I kind of solved that problem, didn't I?"

"You retired," George said.

"I went on emeritus status," Donovan said. "Captain William M. Donovan, Emeritus Catcher of Killers."

"You don't do that sort of thing anymore? Not at all?" Marlowe asked.

"I don't. But things pop into my head from time to time and I call Moskowitz to see if I can make his life miserable the way he made my life miserable for so many years."

Donovan looked at the Miller High Life clock that hovered precariously over the backbar. "Where the hell is Danny?" he asked the clock.

"Your kid is involved in this, too?" George asked.

"Things pop into his head, too. Listen, Richard, do something for me if you can."

"I'll try."

"Tell me about the end-of-the-world party."

George's eyebrows looked like they had been created by a plow.

"You mean, during the Cuban Missile Crisis?"

Donovan said yes.

"What's there to say? A bunch of us sat on the cliff next to what they now call the Franks Library and got drunk. You know, in celebration of the day of reckoning."

"The day we all were to go glowing into that good night," Donovan said.

"Rage, rage against the dying of the light," George said, raising his beer mug in a toast to the ceiling.

"Where'd you get that from?" Donovan asked, astonished.

"Dylan Thomas, of course," George said.

"What, did they print it on the sports page?"

George advised his old friend to fuck himself.

"The day the world was to go blam," Donovan said. "But it didn't."

Marlowe said, "It's too bad you were too young. The party was right up your alley."

"Who was there?"

"Oh, man, it was *so long ago.* I was there. Jake."

Jake Nakima was one of Donovan's closest buddies when he lived in the old neighborhood, a genuine West Side authentic. He was a genial Japanese immigrant who, as a child in California, found himself interned with other Japanese after the attack on Pearl Harbor. As an adult in New York, he amused bar friends by claiming to be the only kamikaze pilot to have flown twenty-nine missions. Sometimes without provocation and while sitting alone, he would hoist a glass and say, "twenty-nine missions," and toast himself.

The end of the world was familiar turf.

"Picciotto Senior," Marlowe added.

Anthony Picciotto Sr. was the local mob money launderer. In pursuit of his career he ran a succession of restaurants that were, on paper, full-bore flops. Through them, however, passed an avalanche of currency that often disappeared because Picciotto claimed he was getting charged $500 for a wad of pizza dough.

He always felt himself near the end, too. Whenever he was to dine in an unfamiliar restaurant, the first thing he did—after sexually harassing the girl up front, that is—was to locate the back door, reconnoiter the alley, and insist on a table near it.

"A guy never knows when he's gonna have to leave in a hurry," he told Donovan once.

"Who else?" the Captain asked.

"I don't know. The usual suspects. It was forever ago. I'll have to give it some thought. Why is it important?"

Donovan shrugged and said that he didn't know.

"What's with the Cuban Missile Crisis?" George asked.

"I got curious, that's all. I was in the Franks Library looking up stuff about McGowan—"

"The guy who could help Danny," George said.

"And—"

He stopped at the sight of a large red custom van that had just double-parked outside the bar. He smiled.

"Whazzat?" George asked, "Paddywagon?"

Donovan shook his head. "Dannywagon," he replied.

He put down his almost entirely untouched beer and edged toward the door.

"You want that?" George said, indicating the bottle.

Donovan shook his head.

"Another chump," George replied, grabbing the bottle and pulling it near.

As he went out the door, Donovan waved his hand and said, "Anon."

"Good to see you again, William," Marlowe said.

"Don't hurry back," George yelled.

7. THE SOUND OF
HOOFBEATS, FLEEING WAR

"Hi, Daddy," the boy called, and Donovan smiled.

After Mary, Donovan's cousin from Ireland and the boy's nanny, lowered the hydraulic lift and helped get the Beast and Danny off it and onto the pavement, Donovan pulled the van into a spot by a rusting old fire hydrant and flipped down the visor, displaying the gold NYPD parking badge.

Then Mary went off on a tour of the local bargain stores, leaving Donovan and son to cross Broadway and make their way up to the main gate of the campus. There was limited parking on that side of Broadway, too, and parked conspicuously by yet another hydrant was a gleaming red Corvette with unmistakable license plates. HEY YO.

"That's Uncle Brian's car!" Danny said.

"Yeah, that sure is it," his father replied.

"Did you know he was going to be here?"

"He's pretty much got to be. Let's see if we can go annoy him."

The shadows were a bit longer when father and son got to the center of the campus, the Beast humming sociably as it rolled along the cobblestones.

A young man and woman were flirting in the shadow of the King statue, but the sight of an adorable young boy in a wheelchair apparently made them queasy and they moved away. Donovan put a hand on his son's shoulder, gave it a little squeeze, and said, "Okay, where are we?"

Danny uttered an uncertain little "unh," then looked around, up, and down, and said, "That's the library over there."

He pointed at the faux Greek facade of the Franks Library, where they were the day before. Then he asked, "Do you mean about the tunnels?"

Donovan nodded.

"We're above the Hub, that big round room where I said it would be great to play dodgeball, remember?"

Donovan remembered, and said so.

Then he asked, "And where is the chapel that Mr. Keogh talked about?"

"There," the boy said, whipping the Beast into a fast ninety and pointing. What he pointed at was a tiny church, half hidden behind an exoskeleton of English ivy. That thick covering of deep green made the chapel hard to see despite its location beside the main gate.

"Good job," Donovan said.

"Is that a church?"

"Yep. Want to go inside?"

"No, I don't think so."

"Me either. Look. How many tunnels are there meeting at the Hub?" Donovan asked.

"Eight."

"We know where two of them go. There and there."

He pointed at the library and then the chapel.

"Where do the others go?" Donovan asked.

The boy once again spun the chair, all in a complete circle this time.

"There," he said, pointing at the administration building, which was laid out north to the library's south. St. Andrew Avolino's Chapel was directly east.

Father and son turned as one, and looked to the west.

"What's that building?" Donovan said out loud.

"I don't know."

"Lemme see." He reached into a back pocket and took out a wad of folded-over papers—a map of the campus, a flyer detailing the library's various collections and hours, a glossary of basic neurological terms, and a Chinese takeout menu. He unfolded the map and peered at it for a moment, then handed it to his son.

The boy peered at it and said, "Okay, west of the Hub is the Human . . . Humanities Institute. I think that's what it says. Daddy?"

"That's it," Donovan said.

"What's humanities?"

"Lotsa stuff. Language, music, literature, philosophy, unpaid student loans, other stuff."

"All in that one building?"

"It does seem like a tight fit, doesn't it," Donovan said. "Maybe they used the Classic Comics version. We used them in high school. I'll show you one someday." He thought for a moment, then said, "I suppose there's some meaning in the humanities being over there staring at the chapel." He pondered again and said, "Maybe not. Okay, I'm looking at the map. And what's to the southwest of the Hub?"

Danny said, "The map says fine arts. Is that like painting?"

"Painting, and sculpture, and maybe photography," Donovan said. "You're a good painter."

"Thanks!"

"I like that one you did of the subway car. Okay, what's southeast?"

"Physics."

Donovan made a frustrated sort of noise, then said, "What's that? Hmm, okay . . . it's . . . ah, let's Google it."

"You *know*, Daddy," the boy said. "You're just saying that because—"

"Because you know more science than I ever will? Has nothing to do with it. When I was in high school I could have told you what physics is. Was. It was about how the Earth stays in orbit around the Sun or how if you drop something off that building over there . . ."

He tilted his head in the direction of the administration building.

"Off that building, the one with the clock way high up there where the pigeons live. If you drop something off the building, it speeds up by thirty-two feet per second until it goes splat on the pavement."

Danny laughed. "That's right."

"But now physics is about atoms and how they move around. Your turf. Me, I have to Google it. Which is what I'll do when I get home. So anyway, the Physics Department is only the first three floors. The other floors are biology, etcetera."

He bent and peered at the map, which his son held in his lap.

"Up to the northeast is law and to the northwest is journalism. Hmm, they put the reporters next to fine arts people. I'm not so sure about that. Anyway, the rest of the buildings are off the quad. They're not important."

"Why not?"

"They're not connected by tunnels like these are."

Danny said, "Okay."

"And all the tunnels come to this point, right under this statue."

"Yeah."

Donovan swept his arm about the area around the sculpture, above the Hub, and said, "What's wrong with this picture?"

"What do you mean, Daddy?" the boy replied.

"I don't know what I mean. There's something wrong with this place. You tell me."

"I don't understand," the boy said. His father sensed that he was both perplexed and flattered.

"Just look. Take a spin around."

Danny said "yeah" and headed off in the Beast, making a circle around the statue. He was about where the walls of the Hub would be if they came all the way up.

The couple that had walked away before had taken interest and were staring.

Then Danny rolled back up to his father and said, "The bricks are different."

"That's right, they are. I was wondering if I was wrong."

"Remember when we went to Coney Island?"

Donovan remembered.

"The boardwalk. The wood on the boardwalk."

"The planks are in this fishbone pattern. But where they intersect with the straight pattern they look off. I mean, in Coney Island they're *supposed* to be off. Come to think of it, everything in Coney Island is a little off. Everything in *Brooklyn* is a little off."

"What you said would make Uncle Brian mad," Daniel laughed.

"He's heard me say it plenty of times before," Donovan said. "Anyway, there the patterns are deliberately off, but here they're supposed to match up and they don't."

"The bricks around the statue don't line up. The man who put them in tried to get it right, but he made mistakes."

"I also think the bricks are newer," Donovan said.

"Me, too. Is this important, Daddy?"

"Probably not. I was just wondering. Why the area about the Hub—*right above* the Hub—is different. Why it was put in at a later time."

Danny didn't say anything.

Donovan said, "Well, a guy notices stuff like this. Why, I can't tell you. I've always done it. You, too. I noticed that I'm gonna need help around here if I get anywhere trying to find Patrick McGowan."

"You don't have to, Daddy," Daniel said. "I'm okay."

Donovan tried to think of something to say, came up dry, and then heard a familiar voice.

"Hey, yo!," it said.

The voice came out of the lengthening shadow of the King statue.

"We've stumbled into a license-plate recitation," Donovan said, turning to face his old partner.

Mosko said, "If it ain't Donovan and Son. Hiya, boys."

"Hi, Uncle Brian," Danny said, turning the Beast toward him.

"You guys are on your way *into* or *out of* the library, I'm sure of that. You got nothing else on your minds."

"Absolutely," Donovan replied, trying to hide a smile but doing a pretty poor job of it, he was certain.

"We were looking at the bricks above the Hub," Danny said proudly.

Mosko smiled in a way that did a poor job of masking a scowl, Donovan was sure, which made *him* smile, quite openly this time.

"The bricks are newer," Danny said.

"Uh, yeah, newer," Mosko said. "I noticed that. Look, on the subject of the tunnels, you want to hear what I found out?"

"If you insist," Donovan said.

"The tunnel from the library was dug first. This was almost a century ago, and it went straight to the administration building."

"For?"

"Bad weather."

"They dug a tunnel"—Donovan scrutinized the distance between the two buildings—"all that way so they didn't have to open umbrellas?"

Mosko said, "Hey, what do I know? They're smarter than us. You and me never went to college, and Danny ain't ready for Harvard yet."

"Columbia," Donovan corrected.

"Yeah, in your old neighborhood, before all your old buddies moved their asses up to West Harlem to escape high rents. These college types are the ones with the brains, and they didn't want to get them rained on. You heard of the ivy tower?"

"I think you mean ivory tower, but go on. There's one over there, by the way." Donovan hooked a thumb over his shoulder at St. Andrew Avolino's Chapel.

After giving it a cursory glance, Mosko said, "This is the ivy tunnel." He pointed down at the ground.

"They dug a tunnel to walk in," Donovan said. "When, exactly?"

"They started digging in 1914. Why is the exact date important? No, don't tell me. Twenty-five years later—"

"Nineteen thirty-nine," Danny said.

"They began the second tunnel," Mosko said.

"Important," Donovan said. "Why?"

"Never mind. I'm probably wrong."

"No shit. You ought to spend more time in the library. The second tunnel crosses the first."

"From where to where did it go?" Danny asked.

"From the humanities building to the chapel."

"I sense they were praying for the future of the human species," Donovan said.

"What?" Mosko asked.

"Nineteen fourteen was the start of World War One. Nineteen thirty-nine was the start of World War Two. You know, that little pas-de-destruction on the other side of the pond."

"Oh," Mosko said, impatient with the Captain's casual forays into the obscure.

Danny had long since learned not to bother asking his father to explain what he meant when he got that way. Danny thought his father was funny, even when he didn't understand why.

Mosko continued, saying, "A little while later, in 1945, they began the tunnel running southeast to northwest. From physics to engineering."

"Pretty much the way that science itself was running in 1945," Donovan said.

"What?"

"I hear the sound of hoofbeats, fleeing war."

"Oh, you mean—"

"Wars. Two of 'em. Atomic bomb explosions, two of 'em shot off in anger. So far."

Donovan added, "When did they dig the next tunnel? No, don't tell me—1963."

"Four," Mosko corrected. "But they started in three."

"Right after the end-of-the-world party," Donovan said.

Sighing, Mosko said, "You hear the sound of hoofbeats. I hear the sound of another stupid Donovan escapade."

"I was too young. But my friends were there."

"What friends?" Mosko asked suspiciously.

"Marlowe. Jake. A few others."

"Christ, the core of the Brendan Behan Fan Club. Don't tell me that you guys are getting back together. Wait! I saw the Dannywagon parked in front of a bar!"

Donovan looked down at the bricks.

"No," Mosko said in a soft wail. "Not again! *No mas!*"

"The bricks above the Hub are *definitely* newer," Donovan said.

"Who's the bartender?"

Trying to ignore the inevitable, Donovan asked when the Hub was dug.

"No, no, no, not *him!*"

"When was the fucking Hub dug?"

Mosko said, "At the same time as the 1964 tunnel."

Donovan looked up, smiled, and said, "It's a goddam fallout shelter, isn't it? The whole damn thing is a fallout shelter."

Mosko said, "How do I know? I only know the dates. Look, I realize I'm keeping you from your scholarly pursuits, but would you like to hear about the *delicti* of the *corpus?*"

Donovan nodded, then bent over his son and said, "Why don't you take another look at the bricks while Uncle Brian and I talk?"

"Daddy, you *explained* to me what happened to that man."

"Humor me, okay?"

Grumbly and a bit testy, the boy spun his chair around, drove back to the statue in the center of the campus, and pondered it for a second. Then he turned slowly around, looking at each building in turn and winding up staring at St. Andrew Avolino's Chapel. Then he drove off to resume circling the statue at about where the new brick met the old, but in the opposite direction.

"Let's hear it," Donovan snapped.

"Hey, whoa! This is a *courtesy* here."

Donovan apologized.

"It was a brick, all right. He was hit from behind, and the blow caused major shit in his brain."

"I love these scientific descriptions," Donovan said. "Single-handedly, you could bring an episode of *CSI* to its knees. Okay, 'major shit in his brain' it is. What else?"

"It looks like he was hit from behind while getting up. There was dust from the floor of the Hub on his knees, and a corresponding patch where the dust was disturbed on the floor. No matter how clean it appears, there was dust. Also, Paz got hit on the lower back of his skull, on the right side."

"Right-handed killer," Donovan said.

"Yep."

"What the hell was he doing on his knees, praying? Gregorio Paz, what were you *doing* to make someone mad enough to kill you?"

"It doesn't seem to be a woman thing or anything like that."

"Those are usually knife-or-gun crimes," Donovan said.

Mosko nodded.

"The vic lived alone in a studio for which he paid next to nothing. In it there's a TV, a VCR, some clothes, a stack of magazines—"

"What did he read?"

"Nothing out of the ordinary. *Time, Newsweek,* that sort of thing. Some papers—*El Diaro, Hoy,* and the *Daily News,* all neat piles on the coffee table. The TV was tuned to the History Channel, if that means anything. There also was a shelf of back copies of *National Geographic,* all carefully arranged by date and lined up so well it might have been done using a ruler. Did you ever see a single guy's apartment that wasn't a wreck? You know, like your old one."

Donovan shrugged. His interest was elsewhere, and he peered around his friend's massive chest. Danny had stopped circling and was talking to a white-haired little old man in a dark suit.

"I doubt it means anything," Donovan said.

"One other thing," Mosko continued. "Paz was a faithful employee with one exception. In the past six or seven months he got three warnings from his boss for being off the job."

"Maybe he was in the Rosa Blanca."

"Whazzat?"

"The bar across the street."

"What, hangin' with the expats from the Upper West Side? I don't think so. What happened is he was supposed to be cleaning in another building someplace—"

"Is that what he did, clean?" Donovan asked.

"Yeah. He was the one who cleaned up the tunnels. He volunteered for the job and took months, but that was okay because he kind of creeped everyone out."

"How so?"

"He wasn't friendly, he never talked, and . . . how do I say this so a New Yorker can understand . . . he liked the job. Loved the job. How many guys who clean basements in this town love their jobs?"

"You never know who's living next to you," Donovan said, projecting faint interest.

"He also normally did exactly what he was told as soon as he was told it. Normally that might be polishing the windows somewhere, and instead he was down in the tunnels poking around. This is *after* he cleaned it so well you could eat off it."

"Really?" Donovan said, a bit more interested but not entirely drawn from keeping an eye on his son.

"Yeah, his boss said he was obsessed with it. He doesn't know why on earth this nothing-of-a-campus-fixit-guy would be so interested in the tunnels."

"Well," Donovan said, smiling and pointing until Mosko turned around. "Why don't we ask Samuel Franks?"

8. A VERY PLEASANT FELLOW
WHO DISAPPEARED ONE DAY

Danny was demonstrating the Beast's braking mechanism when the two men got over there. Danny smiled. "This is Franks. This is my daddy and Uncle Brian."

Donovan took the old man's hand and said, "Captain William Donovan, NYPD."

"Emeritus," Mosko added, introducing himself and shaking Franks' hand.

"I'm glad to meet you," he said in a slightly wobbly voice that carried the slightest hint of a Eastern European accent. "But please don't call me 'Doctor.' I don't give out pills. None of us like to be called 'doctor.' "

"Who's us?" Mosko asked.

"Physicists. Scientists in general. Please just call me 'Franks.' "

"Okay," Mosko replied.

"I was asking your son about this marvelous chair. He was showing me how it operates. It's just wonderful. Rather like the one Stephen Hawking uses."

"His is more complicated," Donovan said.

Franks gave the Captain a look that suggested he was surprised that a policeman, emeritus or not, would know of the Cambridge University professor who refined Einstein's theory of the way the universe works.

Franks looked over his shoulder at a woman whom Donovan had just come to notice. She was fortyish, attractive in a stern sort of way, and dressed in what looked to be an expensive beige pants suit.

He said, "Do you hear that, Dr. Riggs? I *told* you that Hawking's stuff was too complicated."

She smiled wanly, but approached to shake hands after Donovan instigated introductions. She was, he would learn, Marion Riggs, RN, PhD, Franks' constant companion.

"Dr. Riggs is my keeper," he said.

"I am your *nurse*, Professor," she said.

"I thought you guys don't call each other 'doctor' because it makes you sound like you're pushing pills," Mosko said.

"She *is* pushing pills," Franks said.

"Anything with street value attached?" Donovan asked idly.

"I'm only here to make sure that you remain healthy," the woman said.

"And to keep quiet," Franks added. "They don't like it when I talk too much."

"They?" Mosko asked.

"Oh, the university, everyone," he replied, sweeping his arm around the campus. "And I don't blame them a bit. I am a doddering old fool who acts out and is apt to say anything when he doesn't get his way. For example, I would like to ask the young man . . ."

He turned his attention to Danny, bent forward slightly, and said, "Do you mind if I ask, I mean . . ."

"I don't have Lou Gehrig's disease," Danny said. "I don't have anything. I can't walk, that's all. My dad is upset about it."

Smiling faintly, Donovan said, "We've been trying to track down a man who used to teach here. Patrick McGowan."

"Of course," Franks said quickly. "Nice man. I liked him. Now, about the chair. Would you show me how the steering works?"

As the Captain recovered his composure, Danny said, "I use this joystick." He showed Franks the stick, which stuck out of the right armrest. "I can turn it real quick. The turning radius is only two feet. And the Beast can go almost five miles an hour."

"The Beast? You call it 'The Beast'? I think that's wonderful."

"And it can go twenty-five blocks on a full charge. That means I can go all the way to Chinatown and back."

"He likes sliced pork with Chinese vegetables," Donovan said. "Now, about McGowan."

"Oh, I haven't seen him in years. Brilliant man, everyone said. Approaching something important, I hear. I don't know much about his field. All I can tell you is that he was a very pleasant fellow who disappeared one day."

"Just like that?" Donovan asked.

Franks tossed his hands up and made a sound that Donovan took to mean "who knows?"

"He studied stem cells."

"Oh yes, another area about which I know very little. Would like to, though. Are you studying it?"

"Not as much as he should," Mosko cut in.

Donovan said yes.

"My Lord, it goes back to the early 1980s, with McGowan. Something promising regarding nerve damage, I think."

"Spinal cord injury," Donovan said.

"I can't say when we began looking at that," Franks said.

Donovan knew that, to a scientist, "we" meant any colleague, no matter how different a field.

"In the late 1970s, more or less," Donovan said.

"There you have it. You know more about it than me. Well, I hope you find McGowan. I can introduce you to other members of the faculty if you like. Maybe someone will have a better idea."

"I would love that," Donovan said. "And I would *appreciate* it very much."

"Tomorrow night is the monthly reception at Faculty Club.

Most senior faculty show up for the free wine and cheese. Why don't you join me?"

"I'd be honored, Professor."

" 'Franks.' Please."

"All right," Donovan smiled.

Franks and the Captain exchanged cards, a ritual that made Mosko nervous for the time it took. Finally he said, "If I can get a word in here, before the Captain goes back to the library to *continue his research,* what do you know about the tunnels beneath the campus?"

"The tunnels? Down there?" He pointed down.

"Yeah, those."

"And that round thing in the middle? Well, we use them for storage. Boxes of papers and things like that."

"Dissertations," Donovan said.

"Big space wasters, dissertations," Franks said. "I believe it was Einstein who said, 'Don't keep anything you can look up.' But maybe it was someone else who said that."

"Were the tunnels ever used for anything else?" Mosko asked.

"Well, to walk through, of course. When it rained. And in dire circumstances . . ." He laughed. "To go under the feet of the Vietnam War protests."

Donovan smiled. He had been at some at Columbia, in his then role as a rookie police officer assigned to keep order. But order was, by nature, never one of his interests, and he wound up mostly watching the demonstrations.

"Were the tunnels ever used as fallout shelters?" Donovan asked.

"Of *course* they were," Franks replied, laughing rather loudly. "President Townsend was a nervous nellie."

Mosko asked, "President . . . ?"

"George Townsend. President of Riverside University for, oh, I don't know, for forever. From the war until quite recently.

Around 1990, I think. Right after the fall of the Berlin Wall. I think he finally calmed down when the Soviet Union collapsed. I think we all did. He once ordered the tunnels be used as fallout shelters. It caused quite a fuss around here, as you can imagine. Fallout shelters were ridiculous wastes of time."

"Rearranging deck chairs on the *Titanic*," Donovan said.

"A better analogy would be an ostrich hiding its head in the sand in the face of a firestorm. The result would always be—"

"Barbequed ostrich butt," Mosko cut in.

"When the fallout shelter idea was scrapped, the tunnels went back to being used for storage."

"And the Hub was?"

"As you said, it once was a place for everyone to hide from fallout, of course. Everyone being upper administration and prominent faculty including, I'm embarrassed to say, me."

Donovan nodded. "And then?"

"Storage," Franks replied.

Mosko continued, saying "We're—*I'm* investigating the murder of Gregorio Paz."

"The young man whose body was found in the tunnel by the library," Franks said. "I heard about that. He was murdered?"

"Hit with a brick."

"He was a good man. Quiet and respectful. A bit too respectful, if you ask me. He insisted on calling me 'Professor.' "

"And you didn't like that," Mosko said.

"It's preferable to 'Doctor.' I didn't like it anyway. But I couldn't get him to stop."

"It seems unusual for a cleaning man to have so much to do with a person of your stature," Donovan said.

The old man shrugged. "He was always around, cleaning up after me. After *us*. Scientists may be scrupulous about their experiments, but not necessarily so about their floors. He was always there for us."

"That must have been comforting," Donovan said.

"It was, and frankly, we like *quiet*, at least when we're working."

Franks yawned then, and said, "It's time for me to go. I always have tea this time of day at Faculty Club. You'll join me there for the faculty reception tomorrow, Donovan?"

Donovan said that he would.

"One more thing," Mosko said. "Do you have any idea why Paz was poking around in the tunnels?"

"I can't help you. All I can say is that his death is a shame. Catch the man who killed him, will you."

"I promise," Mosko said.

With that the little old man patted Danny on the shoulder, offered an additional few words of praise for the Beast, and scurried off, his keeper keeping close and wary watch.

When Franks was safely out of earshot, Mosko said, "*That* little guy designed the A-bomb?"

"He was one of many scientists working on it."

"He looks like a Polish haberdasher."

"Yeah, a Polish haberdasher with a Nobel Prize and a PhD nurse."

"You noticed that too, eh?" Mosko said. "I guess it's one of the perks of fame."

Donovan said, "Finish briefing me on what happened to Paz. Minus the gore, if you don't mind."

"*Briefing* you?" Mosko said. "Did you hear that, Danny? He wants me to brief him. Okay, I'll humor your dad. We found the brick."

"Where?"

"In the chapel."

"Where in the chapel?"

"In a pile of bricks in the basement, in the crypt."

Danny looked puzzled, so Donovan told him that was a basement or hidden chamber beneath a church.

"Is it connected to the tunnel?" the boy asked.

Mosko nodded. "The tunnel comes out smack in the wall of the crypt. Like everything else below this campus, the tunnel to the crypt is filled with crap."

"More records?" Donovan asked.

Mosko said, "Yeah, and also a stack of copies of *The Book of Common Prayer* and a ton of protest leaflets."

"Protesting what? Vietnam?"

"Only a couple that old. These are mostly environmental stuff, People for the Ethical Treatment of Animals—no Pam Anderson photos, though—and things about how the Patriot Act is trampling our liberties."

"Imagine that," Donovan said.

"The brick was shoved under some other bricks, so I can't tell if the perp was trying to hide it and did a lousy job or wasn't really trying. But Bonaci confirmed it's the murder weapon. And, yes, it's one of the newer bricks."

"Do you know where it came from?" Donovan asked.

Mosko shook his head. "*That* we're still looking for," he said.

"Maybe it came from that pile," Danny said.

"It's one of the things we're looking at. One thing I know, according to Keogh there ain't no other piles of red brick on this campus, at least not that he knows about."

Donovan tugged at his ear, then said, "The killer followed Paz down into the crypt and into the tunnel, pausing only to pick up a brick to hit him with."

"Not bad," Mosko said.

"Can we go down and look?" Danny asked.

"On your way back to the library, sure," Mosko said. "This way."

9. "TURN ME OVER, I AM DONE ON ONE SIDE"

He led them back across the quad and in the front entrance to St. Andrew Avolino's Chapel. There was a ramp for the handicapped, which Danny roared up on the Beast. The dark-stained oak door was heavy, and swung open with what seemed to Donovan only a bit less effort than it required to open the door behind which he found Paz. Danny led the way inside.

Two rows of golden oak pews glowed faintly in the final rays of the day coming through a circular stained glass window above the entrance to the multi-faith church. Amidst a flurry of gold and brown leaves and branches, a majestic figure of the sixteenth-century Italian priest and lawyer St. Andrew Avolino, the patron saint of Sudden Death. He was also the patron saint of Sicily and stood holding a book that had an unfortunate resemblance to a slice of Sicilian pizza.

The rest of the church was rather conventional. The row between the pews led up to a plain Congregational altar that in another circumstance might have been a long chopping block.

To one side, and a bit forward, was a similarly stark lectern, and on the other side was an organ, its pipes beckoning the ceiling like marsh reeds. A plain gold cross took up most of the wall behind.

The vestry was a bit warmer, decorated as it was with pre-Raphaelite reproductions, lithographs of European cathedrals, and charcoals of two young boys whom Donovan took to be the rector's sons. Two slatted doors opened on as many racks of vestments. Down the west wall from them was the door to the stairs that led down to the crypt.

"Over the years we've spent a lot of time in basements," Mosko said.

"In New York you either go up or down, and down is the better place to hide bodies," Donovan replied.

"Ready for descent, kid?"

"Ready!" Danny said.

Grunting, the two men hefted boy and wheelchair and carried him down a staircase that was never designed for the purpose.

The crypt was made of red brick which, unlike that covering much of the rest of the campus, was darkened by age and moisture untouched by the sun. And unlike the rest of the tunnel system, the crypt held something other than old boxes.

Piled neatly against one wall was detritus of the A-bomb scare—ten large, gray rectangular tins of fallout-shelter survival crackers. The tins were piled neatly by twos, arranged against the wall with labels facing out. Nearby were ten-gallon containers marked "distilled water."

"Whazzis?" Mosko asked, though he must have known.

Even after all those years, and now head of the Department of Special Investigations, Mosko still liked to play the role of Donovan's straight man.

"A relic of irrational fear," Donovan said, "and in a house of worship. *Mon dieu.*"

Danny smiled, though he seemed unsure why.

"There were piles of these supplies in the basement of my old building on Riverside," Donovan continued. "Crackers, water, biscuits. One day a bunch of us got drunk and stole tins of both and opened them in my kitchen."

"You ate those things?" Mosko asked.

"With guacamole. They sucked. I'm not sure that roasting in

nuclear holocaust wouldn't be preferable."

Against the opposite wall was the pile of bricks, now marked off with yellow crime-scene tape.

Mosko pointed at it and said, "This is where we found the murder weapon. It was just shoved under the top layer of bricks almost like the perp didn't care if anyone found it."

"Or was in a hurry to avoid being seen."

"Or was late for class," Danny said.

"A student?" Donovan asked no one in particular.

"Maybe a professor," Mosko said. "Clear plastic was tossed over the pile. The plastic looked like it had been there for years. We took it to the lab to check for prints and other stuff. The bottom of the pile was bricks from early construction. The top of the pile was from the most recent construction. The murder brick was from there. These people don't like to throw anything out."

"They stacked it neatly," Donovan said. "More or less."

"That's Paz's work. His apartment was neat too. But neater than this."

"A touch of obsessive-compulsive disorder, I guess," Donovan said. "But maybe not as hefty a dose of Prozac as needed."

"I keep my room neat," Danny said.

"With Mary's help," his father replied.

Danny said, "Uncle Brian, this pile of bricks isn't as neat as my room."

"No, it isn't," Donovan said.

"And everything else is," Mosko agreed.

"Maybe this is the garbage pile," Danny said.

"Maybe," Donovan said.

Mosko replied, "Didn't I mention that Paz had the job of cleaning up the tunnels?"

"They got the right man for the job."

"Yeah. And when he was done he couldn't let it go. He kept

coming back, even when it got him in trouble."

"Maybe he came back because he forgot something," Danny wondered.

"Or couldn't find something he was sure was there," Mosko said.

"Mercury," Donovan replied.

"Yeah, that," Mosko said. "Let's go take another look to see if we can find it ourselves."

As the three detectives moved down the tunnel leading from the crypt to the Hub, Donovan was struck by the relative newness of the records stored there. True, there were boxes and more boxes, but they were in modern banker's boxes marked with neat labels.

He ran his finger along the row of labels, neatly printed, indicating that the records were placed in chronological order. The most recent—slightly into the 2000s, were outermost. The oldest—1937 to 1939—were closest to the Hub. *Sloppy of me,* Donovan thought. *I didn't look for that in the tunnel where I found the body. I have to go back.*

When the little procession got to the Hub, Danny took off on his own. As if imagining a game of dodge ball, he scooted around the circular cavern, touching the walls, imitating the way his dad explored the boxes moments before.

On his own, the Captain wandered over to one of the pipes that projected slightly from the walls. As when he first saw them, he stuck a finger inside.

"Support structure?" Mosko suggested.

Donovan nodded. "Holding up what?"

"Shelves?"

"Could be."

"Storing the emergency supplies this way doesn't sound right," Mosko continued. "Those tins are too big, and anyway, they look like they were meant for the floor."

"There's other stuff," Donovan said.

"Beds, cots."

"Bunks," Donovan said.

"They stored provisions in the halls," Mosko suggested. "What did they use for a kitchen?"

"I don't think that survival biscuits would require much cooking. What about a toilet?"

"Right here where everyone is sleeping?" Mosko said.

"There's got to be evidence of one someplace," Donovan said. "I'll have to take another look. Toilet plumbing hookups are hard to hide."

"Can *I* go look?" Danny asked, having rolled within earshot.

Donovan shrugged.

"No time like the present," Mosko said. Then he turned to the Captain and said, "You coming along, or are you gonna let me do my job?"

"You handle it alone. You have competent help now." Donovan smiled at his son. "Besides, I want to go back and look in the tunnel where my son and I found the body."

To Danny, he added, "You go and make sure that Uncle Brian does everything right."

"Yeah!" the boy exclaimed.

After emitting a brief and pointless grumble, Mosko smiled at the boy, then clapped him on the back and said, "Let's go, boss."

And off they went.

After the two of them had begun down a new tunnel, Donovan stood alone in the Hub. He looked around, at the pipes and the bricks, and tried to imagine what it might be like to hide in a fallout shelter, imagining oneself safe while men, women, and children were burned alive a handful of feet, and a layer of bricks, above.

He looked at the ceiling. Even from below, the bricks were

76

clearly newer than the rest. Well, he thought, Martin Luther King's statue deserved a solid foundation.

Then the Captain yawned, thought, *Fuck this! Mosko can handle it now that he has help.* And he walked back into the original tunnel to resume looking in boxes.

10. "There was a young man from Nantucket . . ."

The words tumbled off the old pages of notes and records—the ones meticulously printed out on perforated computer paper of the sort that used to suck into the floor-standing printers that dominated offices at the dawn of the PC age, twenty years before. Donovan could hear the whine of the dot matrix printhead zipping out the pages at the breakneck pace of two a minute.

Some of the words were familiar to him, but most were not—coding or noncoding DNA, Hox genes, genetic expression, evo devo—and throughout all the indignities heaped on fruit flies who were genetically manipulated to have feet growing out of their heads instead of antennae.

McGowan's name came up often in the years leading up to the early 1990s. The clues were tantalizing, but maddeningly so. There were bits about "evolutionary developmental biology" (the "evo devo" that had puzzled Donovan for as long as it took to figure out what it meant) and bits about coding for neural development in frogs.

There also was, in what Donovan had come to recognize as McGowan's hand, something a bit off topic:

> *There was a young man from Nantucket*
> *Whose . . .*

A long-ago censor, doubtless a faculty secretary, had taken a ballpoint pen and vociferously blacked out the rest. But Donovan remembered the limerick from the eighth grade and smiled.

So the professor liked the occasional bawdy poem. So much the better, for such would not go unnoticed on a staid university campus. He also doodled Christmas trees, Donovan noted. Little Christmas trees with a ball sitting atop each. They were everywhere, in the margins of everything.

Perhaps other faculty secretaries remembered him.

Maybe he's from Nantucket, Donovan pondered.

Then embarrassment set in, and he banished the thought. He closed his notepad and returned the box of records to its place along the tunnel wall. He put away his Maglite, which he had been using to augment the light from the bulbs that hung like bats along the tunnel ceiling.

He went and found Danny, rolling out of a tunnel with Mosko lagging behind. Maybe he was imagining it, but Donovan thought that Mosko looked a little worn out from following the boy and the Beast around.

"How you holding up?" Donovan called from across the Hub.

"Your kid gets around pretty good," was the reply.

"Tell me about it."

"We found where the bathroom was," Danny said. He was beaming.

"Where?" Donovan asked.

"Down the tunnel leading to the journalism building," Mosko said, smiling faintly.

Donovan giggled. His battles with reporters were legendary.

"About twenty feet down the tunnel and on the left side there's—was—a hookup," Mosko said. "It was set in kind of an alcove that since has been bricked up. Danny found it."

"The bricks are different," the boy said.

"There's an epidemic of that around here," Donovan offered, again casting his eyes ceilingward. His gaze lingered there long enough to be noticed.

"Whaddya see?" Mosko asked.

"There's something wrong."

Mosko looked up. "The bricks are different there, too. People rebuild all the time. So what?"

"So I don't know," Donovan said. "I'm getting tired of this, and want to go home."

"Good. Goodbye."

"I'm hungry," Danny offered.

"I don't think this tunnel shit is leading anywhere," Mosko said. "Paz was killed because this is where he happened to be."

"Sounds good to me," Donovan agreed.

"The bricks where the toilet used to be are new because they no longer needed this ant farm for a fallout shelter after they held the party, and the world didn't end," Mosko said. "The bricks here around the statue"—he pointed up—"are new because the statue is new. That is, newer than when the statue went up. That was 1968, probably. Your favorite year."

"It hurts my brain to think about 1968. I wonder what was here before they tore it down to put up the statue. Well, that should be easy enough for you to find out. Danny and I are going home."

His son smiled and put the pedal to the metal—that's what he called it—and spun the chair in a neat 360.

"Forget the tunnels," Mosko said. "I'm gonna go take another look at the vic's personal life. There's got to be a relative or neighbor or some other homicidal maniac in there."

"Happy hunting," Donovan said.

He listened vaguely while rinsing the dishes and putting them in the washer, scented by the lingering aroma of curry and coconut milk.

Marcie was nearing the end of a days-end rant, saying, "So the whole thing came down to a dog. To a *dog!*"

"Pit bulls aren't dogs," Donovan said. "They're fuses awaiting a match."

"Tell it," she replied.

"Pit bulls are bought by guys who want to hurt someone. Who? I don't know, the world maybe. But they don't have the balls to do it themselves. So they buy the fuse, feed it some kibble, and wait for the unsuspecting passerby to light a match."

"The vic was an *old man*," Marcie said, taking over the rinsing chore from her husband and sliding the bowl in his hand into the washer.

"Seventy?" Donovan asked. "Eighty?"

"Eighty-*two*. All he did was stop to pet the dog and the damn thing *mauled* him."

"Did he die?"

"*Yes*," Marcie said, a bit sharply. "Do you mean you don't *remember?* It was only six months ago and was on all the channels. No, of course, if it isn't in the *Times* it doesn't exist for you."

"I was preoccupied," Donovan replied.

She was quiet for a moment, then continued. "The dog ripped his carotid out. He died within minutes."

"And Fido's owner?"

"He was arrested and charged with man one."

"The prosecutor must be ambitious," Donovan said.

She bobbed her head up and down. "He's running for his boss's job."

"That's gotta be pretty rough when it comes time for annual evaluation," Donovan said, walking across the kitchen to the table and lowering himself onto a chair.

"I can't believe you don't remember," Marcie said.

"I've been *busy*," he replied, a bit sharply.

She didn't betray whether or not she noticed. She went on, saying, "I pleaded him down to man two. He's going up for three to five . . . . no, I don't know. Forget I said that."

Then she looked at Donovan and continued, "Don't worry about forgetting it. You weren't listening. You never listen to me anymore."

"And the dog?"

"Destroyed. What's bothering you lately?"

Donovan said that nothing was bothering him.

"How has your research been going?" she asked.

She walked over and sat next to him, pausing just long enough to ruffle his hair and kiss him atop the head. "You're losing a bit more on the top," she said.

"As Brian likes to say—"

" 'Real men don't waste hormones growing hair,' yes, I've heard it before. Over and over. How is he?"

"Good. He's good."

"What's he up to?"

"The body in the basement of the Riverside library. What, you don't know about that? It's been on all the channels."

She took an emotional step backwards, it seemed to him.

"How's his case going?"

"It's going. He's doing a good job. He's doing the right things."

"You trained him well."

"He's making fewer enemies than I did. But then, give him time. A high-profile job like that is pissoffable." That was a word that Donovan made up to describe activities likely to infuriate others.

"Are you involved?"

Donovan shook his head. "Only insofar as our paths cross. I've got enough on my hands. The research is slow. Frustrating."

"Any leads?"

"Tulane was the last good one, and that went nowhere. I

need to spend more time in the library. Another couple of weeks, maybe."

She made an "um" sort of sound.

"I can't believe they're not putting more of it online," he continued. "But there are a lot of personal records in there, though. A lot of things that people don't want the world to see. Bad grades. Bad attitudes."

Her mind perhaps drifting elsewhere, Marcie said, "He never made it to the sentencing."

Donovan looked over. "Who?" he asked.

"The perp. The vic's son killed him. Beat his brains in with a tire iron, right there on the Grand Concourse and One Hundred Eighty-second."

"Irish neighborhood, years ago," Donovan mused. "Who's representing him?"

"Lorenzo Lorber. Know him?"

"No."

"Bronx public defender's office. My office. The son can't afford private counsel, of course. He killed his father's killer."

"Sounds Shakespearean."

"It is, *very*," Marcie said.

"These people have no money and no power and no choice but to do it themselves," Donovan said. "Not that I'm recommending first-person justice."

Marcie gave him a look, then turned her head away to a batch of mail and notes held in a rectangular wicker basket that sat atop the table. Next to it was the vase holding fresh-cut mums from the garden. Mary looked after the garden when she wasn't looking after Danny.

"You got a call," Marcie said, handing her husband a note scribbled on Bronx public defender's office stationery. "First call in two weeks that's been for you. You've really been out of touch since you retired. Until now."

"Who called?" Donovan asked, his interest picking up a notch.

"Marlowe. Richard Marlowe. Your old friend who does puzzles."

"He must need help with something again," Donovan said, though he knew that two requests within one day were unlikely. He snatched the paper from his wife.

"He said that *he* has something for *you*. How did he get back in your life? It's been *years.*"

"It was. Nine or ten. I ran into him today."

"Where?"

"In a bar on Broadway across from the campus. The Rosa Blanca."

Marcie gave him a look, a *look* that could have been wary, or it could have been tired. He couldn't be sure. All he knew was that it had been a long day for her too.

"Want to tell me about it?" she asked.

He didn't.

"When you get ready," Marcie said.

"When you're actually home to listen to me," he said.

She took another emotional step backwards. This one was clear.

"What is it with you lately? What's the matter?"

"*Nothing* is the matter. No, actually that's not true. You see, *I* want to matter, and I don't anymore."

"We *talked* about the long hours I'd have to work," she said, a bit angrily.

"Yeah, we did," he replied. "I talk, I'm a big mouth. You talk, you're a lawyer. I need to talk to my old friends. I'm going there now and see what they want," Donovan announced.

"What do you think that might be?" Marcie asked, slowly and in a flat tone.

"It isn't a puzzle," Donovan said. "It has to be about a party."

She looked at him, away from him, then flashed a smile and

said, "When is it? We'll all go."

"It *was* in 1962," Donovan said.

Marcie's brow imitated a plowed field. She reached a hand in front of her husband's face and made an "out with it" gesture.

"It was an end-of-the-world party," Donovan explained. "It was held in anticipation of the nuclear holocaust that everyone expected to be the coda on the Cuban Missile Crisis. Nineteen sixty-two."

"You were too young to be there," Marcie said.

He shrugged.

"This was in Riverside Park, where *you* used to have *your* parties, I suppose," she said.

"No. It was on the cliff overlooking the Hudson next to the Riverside University campus. It was Marlowe's idea."

"Why is this important *now?*"

"I don't know, but I feel that it is," Donovan said.

"Important to finding McGowan?"

"It's just a feeling."

"Well," she said, emitting a sigh almost strong enough to wobble the wind chimes by the garden door, "you're the one with the strong feelings lately. *You're* the bruised apple in this orchard. Forgive my phrasing something the way you would."

"I'll try not to be late," he said.

"Are you driving?"

"Subway," he said.

"Like the old days."

"Like that."

Marcie said, "Do what you want. I'm going to bed. I have a full day tomorrow."

He looked away as she walked off in silence, and without looking back.

11. THE SHED BLOOD OF
INTERESTING CONVERSATION

Donovan enjoyed watching the sudden and joyous lifting of the cell phone blackout. There had been times, and not so long ago, that the notion of talking on a phone in public with all the world listening repulsed him to the extent that he made Mosko promise to shoot him if he ever did it. Now it seemed like everyone was on the phone all the time. One time, the sound of someone walking down Broadway apparently talking to voices in his head was a sure sign of madness. Now it was a sure sign of wireless technology enabling you to coordinate your Christmas card list with Mom and Dad while you were picking up pizza. Talking on the cell phone was so ubiquitous that the inability to do so inspired madness.

The IRT No. 1 local train had lumbered noisily up and down Broadway for a century (but without ever being called the Broadway local, an honor that fell to the BMT train that went up and down Sixth Avenue; "go figger," Mosko might say). The No. 1 ran from Battery Park all the way north to Van Cortland Park in the Bronx. For nearly the entire duration of its travels through Manhattan, the train was a cell phone nightmare. There was nothing coming over the ether, not even the static that customarily assured radio users that *something*, however useless, was going on.

There was one exception. When the northbound No. 1 rose from the underground just past Columbia University and became an elevated line for ten or so blocks, everyone's cell phones snapped on and there was a desperate grab at connectivity. What old-timers saw as a respite from looking at the yellowing utility lights and deepening shadows underground, cell users saw as a desperate chance to update the Christmas card list.

That was hard to do in thirty seconds, though. And that was about as long as you had after finding the number on the dialer, touching the keypads, and waiting for the thing to connect to the antenna atop a nearby building. Many times, Donovan heard a desperate "Hi. I'm above ground. I—"

And that was the end of it.

Connectivity, Donovan thought as his train crept back below ground on the last leg of his evening trip—the first in a *long* time—to see his old friends. It was *important* to have old friends, ones who knew things and you could rely on. And who never judged.

Upper Broadway smelled of salt air from the river mixed with barbeque smoke from the *parrilladas,* and exhaust from the cars, and oil from the parking spots where it had leaked onto the pavement turning the latter black with that snappy ozone smell from all the electricity in the lights. Shakira was on the speakers in front of the CD shop, and Donovan swore he heard the static crackling from the flashing, broken—he could now see that—neon Corona sign in the window of the Rosa Blanca.

The bar at night awoke from its daylight neighborhood dolor and became the cheaply glistening centerpiece of the block. The sidewalk in front was briskly trafficked with evening shoppers, some of whom, mainly the young boys, stomped on the steel basement doors set flush with the concrete to allow beer deliveries, and sent a crashing sound down the asphalt.

From the open front door of the saloon blared the latest hit from an experimental rock band that, according to the preternaturally gray young man at the record store down

Hudson Street from the Donovan townhouse, was named the Flaming Lips. He found himself mumbling along with a jolly tune about blowing up the world.

Someone thought about the same thing once, he thought, visions of end-of-the-world parties and survival biscuits joining the smell of *parrillada.*

Fearlessly prepared to confront his past and the good neighborhood people who used to live in it, Donovan walked into the bar. He was met with a collective smile, he thought, though he also feared that he imagined it. What he *did* imagine and hope for was an old familiar voice and the hefting of a bottle of Pabst.

"Twenty-nine missions!" it went.

A bunch of them were there, three or four or perhaps seven, his old friends and drinking buddies from the days when he had plenty of both and laughed occasionally, and he was embarrassed but a little glad to look at his reflection in the backbar mirror between the smudged bottles of whiskey and smiled, *I remember this.*

He high-fived two of the smiling faces there to greet him, but sat next to Jake, where he always sat. In preparation for the night landing, Jake flicked some crumbs of Ritz cracker off the stool.

"Sit," he said.

Donovan sat.

He hoisted the bottle of Schmidt that Jake had bought him and called out, "Let this meeting of the night watchmen flame-keepers come to order."

The assembled cheered and laughed, though Donovan suspected most were unaware that he had recently rekindled his decades-old fondness for Tom Waits songs.

The laughter gave way to a somewhat awkward silence, and the captain looked around at the expectant faces and asked

Jake, "What?"

"You left to seek fame and fortune downtown and found it," Jake said. "They want you to buy them drinks."

Donovan laughed, but not as bitterly as one might have expected. "Right. I'm rich. I'm constantly reminded."

"What did you think they would do," Jake said, "congratulate you? Ask how wifey is?"

Donovan stood, emptied two fifties from his wallet onto the bar, then signaled to George by making a circle in the air with a finger and said, "All of 'em."

A cheer rose, and within minutes newly poured, served, or refreshed drinks were being waggled in his direction accompanied by shouts of "Thanks, Bill."

"You won the lottery," Jake said, as Donovan settled back down.

"Fuck I did," he said, quite without thinking about it.

That got him a worried, questioning look. He pretended not to notice, hoping his slip would be misinterpreted as the quiver of a drunk's tongue, which it had been often enough in the past.

"Okay, let's hear it," Jake said. The tone had turned serious, something Donovan had never encountered in the man. He was unsure what to make of it, or what to do about it, and so feigned interest in a moth that was circling a lightbulb.

"Do you see that moth?" he asked, tilting his head in the direction of the insect that was spiraling toward a lightbulb that hung loose from a heat-cracked cord behind and to the left of a dust-covered bottle of raspberry schnapps. Donovan was trying to give the impression that the sum total of his interest was calculating the trajectory of the doomed insect.

"Let's *hear it*," Jake said again.

"Hear what?" Donovan said, giving up.

"*It*," the man insisted, ripping a strip of paper out of the label of his beer bottle, using a thumbnail that was jagged and cracked from decades of picking up trash in Riverside Park.

Donovan found himself forced to admit that the moth could manage to destroy itself quite well without his expert help, thank you.

"What are you asking me and why?" he asked.

"Why are you here?" Jake replied.

Donovan hefted his bottle and tried to rip *his* label, to display comradeship. But his thumbnail, in recent years accustomed to paperwork, not hard labor, had grown a bit soft and wasn't jagged or sharp enough.

"If it wasn't for beer I wouldn't be here," he said, using the soft brogue of a beloved Irish uncle long gone.

Jake said, "Come on, Bill, we've known each other for a long time. It's been ten or fifteen years since you were a regular at this place. Now you show up twice in a day, both afternoon and evening shifts. What gives?"

"I was a regular at a place long since turned into a Starbucks. Had I known that, against all odds and logic, you mugs had reconvened at *another* old dive, forty or fifty blocks uptown in West Harlem, I would have come around more often."

"You mean, if the rich wife *let you*," George said. He hadn't lost his shark's ability to detect the shed blood of interesting conversation.

He walked up, twisting a white bar towel around one hand.

Donovan growled and snapped, loud enough to be heard a distance, "She's busy being a lawyer."

Down the bar, someone—Donovan wasn't sure who— shouted out, "I object!"

"Fuck you all," Donovan said.

"Answer my question," Jake insisted.

"Which is? Oh, why am I here? I was in the neighborhood."

George made a large masturbatory gesture, large enough to

service an ox.

"Where's Marlowe?" Donovan asked. "He left a message at my house."

"He went down the block for a sandwich," George said.

"Do you know what he wants?"

"Ask him," the bartender said, acknowledging the man's return with a sweep of a hand in the direction of a pointedly unoccupied barstool. In common saloon etiquette, you never took the seat of a regular, and newcomers who made that mistake were quickly educated.

"William," Marlowe said, sitting down in front of a white-wrapped chicken salad on rye. "You got my message."

"You remembered my phone number."

"It was smart of you to keep the old one when you moved into Marcie's townhouse."

Donovan thought of saying, "*Our* townhouse," but was grateful when he didn't. What he said was, "It only rings in my study."

That he regretted, but it was too late.

"Your *study*," George said.

"Yes, study, where people read. You heard of reading?"

He picked up the copy of the *Daily News* that was nearby and flipped it over to the back sports page.

"Here," he said, "read."

George went off to serve some other customers or to bring a platter of grief to them, most likely both.

Marlowe had spread the white deli paper out carefully and arranged the sandwich atop it. "I may have something for you," he said.

"What?"

"Your Patrick McGowan."

Donovan's eyes flashed to the moth, which no longer appeared quite so doomed, and then to his friend's face.

"Do you know where he is?" Donovan asked.

"No. But I found someone who knew him pretty well when he was here."

"Who?"

"Michael Yeager, the provost."

"The provost."

"Yes. The man in charge of the faculty and educational affairs. Late Latin, *praepositus,* 'chief.' He wants to meet you."

Donovan looked quizzical. "You told him who I am? Was? Whatever?"

"I didn't have to," Marlowe said, a bit impishly. "He *knew.*"

"Okay," in a tone that meant a "let's hear it" similar to the one Jake asked a little before.

"It seems that twenty-odd years ago he took a seminar in community policing at Columbia Law, and—"

"Oh, *Christ,*" Donovan said. For the first time in a long while, he took a full-bodied swig of beer instead of sipping at it.

"And he was *very* impressed with the adjunct associate professor running it."

"That was the seminar where I met Marcie. She was one of my students."

"I know."

Donovan muttered, "Well, some things turn out better than others."

He hadn't muttered it quietly enough, and Jake gave him a sharp glance.

"That's what you get for sexually harassing your students," Marlowe said.

Donovan *oomphed.*

Then he said, "What does Michael Yeager look like?"

"Oh, round-faced, red hair, about my height—"

"I remember him. He was the middle-aged guy who was dating Marcie when I scooped her up. He must be seventy now. God, it never rains, but it pours. And he still likes me?"

"As a teacher. In fact, I think he wants to offer you a job."

Donovan took another swig.

"You gotta be kidding me."

"The man wants to talk to you about teaching another seminar. He didn't tell me what about, but I assume something to do with detecting."

"Homey don't do that no more," Donovan said.

"You *are* trying to track down Patrick McGowan," Marlowe said.

"Different thing."

"How is it different?"

Donovan reflected, then didn't answer, choosing to let his obvious reflection speak for him.

"William, the man has followed your career. He knows how famous you are. Were. Whatever."

"I'm not famous. The *idea* is famous. The idea of tracking down people, that is. It's the deeply ingrained hunting instinct that's famous, but I seem to be getting skunked in this hunt. Okay, where and when do I meet him?"

Marlowe smiled, and said, "I took the liberty of making an appointment for you. You're retired now, so there can't be too much on your plate."

Donovan growled.

"I mean, you can't have too many *specific appointments.* Tomorrow, at four, you'll come to the faculty reception with me."

"Tomorrow at four Danny will be with me and we'll be in the basement of Franks Library."

"No, you'll be at the Faculty Club with me. Bring Danny. I want to meet him. And he should get used to an academic setting. He may want to go to Riverside. Being your son, he's smart."

"He's *scary* smart. He's begun doing my Google searches for me. And he's very grounded for a ten-year-old in a wheelchair. Not at all like his father."

Donovan watched as Marlowe picked up one half of his sandwich, carefully assuring that no chicken salad escaped the twin slabs of rye.

"Can I have your pickle?" Donovan asked.

Nodding, Marlowe replied, "*May* I have your pickle, William. You're back in academia now."

12. ". . . BEAUTIFUL PEOPLE TO MAKE LOVE TO, GOOD AND TRUE FRIENDS, ROBUST HEALTH, AND FIVE-AND-A-HALF-MILLION-DOLLAR TOWNHOUSES . . ."

Riverside University's Faculty Club was a set out of old English movies, with dark leather armchairs facing an immense brick fireplace. The scent of ashes and brandy flickered in the air as a string quartet played Bach as vested waiters delivered merlot and hors d'oeuvres.

Led by Marlowe, Donovan and son entered the room with feelings halfway between ease and terror. At least that's what Donovan felt, and what was on the boy's mind he couldn't be sure. The youngest Donovan looked happy to be among people he judged to be especially important.

Several of the several dozen in the room glanced at the trio, in particular the smiling boy in the wheelchair, and then looked away. No one looked horrified, which Donovan took to be a good sign. A waiter approached with a tray of merlot, which Marlowe took but Donovan politely declined.

"Can I have a Coke?" Danny asked.

Donovan gave him a look.

"*May* I have a Coke?" the boy asked, with a little smile.

The waiter said he would get one and went off to do so.

"What do you think, William?" Marlowe asked. "Are you comfortable?"

"I haven't seen any of them on wanted posters, so why not? Danny, do you like being here?"

"Sure."

After Danny got his Coke, the trio worked the room, Mar-

95

lowe introducing them around. Everyone was polite. A few were condescending to the boy, which didn't appear to bother him. No one appeared to know who Donovan was, which was fine with him. One or two gave Marlow askance glances, which Donovan assumed was fallout from the common knowledge of his drinking.

Marlowe didn't seem to care.

It was when they got to the open bar—really just a banquet table on which was laid out a supply of wine and snacks—that Provost Yeager approached them, all smile and handshake. He was shorter than Donovan remembered, and heavier, and had less hair, of course, but appeared reasonably jolly.

"Captain Donovan!" he exclaimed, taking Donovan's hand and pumping it.

A bit too eagerly for an academic, Donovan thought, and then he wondered why he thought that. There wasn't a mold for them, was there?

"Bill Donovan," he replied.

"And son?" He looked down at Danny.

"Hi, I'm Danny," the boy replied, and his hand was shaken too.

"Your only child?"

"My youngest son. The other one is working today. How have you been?"

"Wonderful, thank you. This is a wonderful university with a wonderful faculty. I'm honored to be part of it. And I'm honored to see you again, my old teacher."

"I don't think that running one seminar counts as having been a teacher," Donovan said.

"Of course it does. And how is Marcie? I read about the marriage? In Times Square at midnight on New Year's Eve? You certainly have a flair for the dramatic."

"Had. I'm retired."

"I *heard* that, from Richard."

Marlowe nodded, and raised his glass as one used to tip his hat in the old days.

"I know why you're here, and maybe I can help. But first, first . . ." He smiled in emphasis of the point. "I would like you to consider teaching another seminar."

Donovan shook his head. "That was a one-time deal," he said. "I wasn't any good at it and I felt awkward."

"Far from the truth."

"I don't feel comfortable standing in front of a group of people and spouting absolutes. There's no one way of doing anything."

"Then spout *that*," Yeager said.

"Besides, I'm busy. I'm doing something, which is why I'm here."

"In a moment. But . . . surely you have ideas on crime and society. On the criminal mind . . ."

"*The?*" Donovan said.

"On criminal *minds* and society. On what makes the respectable person different from the disrespectable person."

"Possessions," Donovan said.

"Possessions?" Yeager asked.

Marlowe, who may have guessed where Donovan was going, offered a wisp of a smile.

"Yes, possessions. Nice cars, good incomes, wonderful sons"—he placed a hand on Danny's shoulder—"beautiful people to make love to, good and true friends, robust health, and five-and-a-half-million-dollar townhouses . . ."

Marlowe's wispy smile became less so.

"It's possible to do without some of those without becoming disrespectable, if you even care," Donovan said. "Look, I'm flattered by the offer, but no thanks. If you want me to swing by for a guest lecture, that's one thing. Can—*may* we talk about

Patrick McGowan?"

"Of course," Yeager said, manfully hiding disappointment. "What do you want to know?"

"First, where do you think he is?"

"I have no idea. He didn't show up for class one day. Didn't say goodbye. No forwarding address. Nowhere to send paychecks to, and there were a good number before we finally took him off the payroll. Never cleaned out his apartment."

"No suicide note?" Marlowe asked idly.

"None that ever came to my attention. And I was vice-provost in charge of the science faculty in those days. I saw quite a lot of him, too."

"What did you think of the man?" Donovan asked.

"Brilliant," Yeager said, with an of-course twist of the lips. "Of course, I personally know nothing about his field of interest—stem cells—except that they've been much in the news lately."

"My interest is in neurogenic stem cells," Donovan said. "Those are the—"

Danny interrupted, asking, "Can I go get one of those little hot dogs?"

"Sure. Don't run over anyone's foot."

"I'll be careful, Dad," the boy said as he rolled off.

"The ones that grow into nerve fibers," Donovan continued, nodding in the direction of his son.

"I see," Yeager replied. "Pardon my asking, but—"

"Both legs, both paralyzed, unknown etiology." Donovan loved the phrase "unknown etiology," for it was much better than a Brooklynish "who knows?"

"Everything else works, including his brain, which is better than mine."

"That *was* McGowan's field," Yeager continued. "That's where all his publications were. He studied stem cells in some kind of frog."

"*Xenopus,*" Donovan said.

Yeager said, "I really am not sure."

"African clawed frog. Unpleasant-looking critter. A pancake with feet."

"I kept hearing that McGowan was a candidate for a Nobel. That's all nonsense, of course, because the Nobel Prize is special. You can't lobby for it. It tends to come twenty years after your work has been demonstrated to have been of great value. And you don't know it's coming."

"Apart from the Swedish camera crews suddenly taking an interest in how you furnish your apartment," Marlowe said.

"Which reminds me," Donovan said, "may I see his lab?"

"Of course, what remains of it. The physical setting is still there, but all the equipment is different. And the woman who runs it now is studying snails."

"I know. I read up on her."

"It has something to do with cancer," Yeager said.

"Their toxin is cytotoxic. It kills cells by disrupting DNA. Cancer is out-of-control cell growth."

Marlowe said, "One scientist researches how cells grow, and his replacement studies how they die. That's a neat kind of symmetry."

"I'd also like to see his apartment," Donovan said. "I understand he had one owned by the university."

"Of course he did. It's on the Gold Coast."

"The stretch of Riverside Drive where the university keeps the posh apartments used to attract faculty who otherwise would go work at Princeton."

"We wouldn't *hire* anyone who would consider teaching at Princeton," Yeager sniffed.

"Do you know who has it now?" Donovan asked.

"*I* do."

Donovan's eyes narrowed.

"Well, I *am* provost," Yeager said. "It entitles you to certain perks. Come over anytime. I can tell you that no evidence remains of his having lived there."

"I'd like to see it anyway."

Yeager shrugged, and then smiled as Danny returned, holding a plate of hors d'oeuvres in one hand while steering the Beast with the other.

"I got us some food," he announced proudly.

Donovan and Yeager said thanks, but no thanks, and Marlowe had a Triscuit that was adorned with a smoked oyster over which cheddar had been melted.

The lull in the conversation was tempting, and Danny gave in. He said, "May I ask Mr. Yeager a question?"

All eyes were on him.

"Sure," the provost replied.

"Did anyone ever play dodgeball in the Hub?"

Yeager laughed, and Donovan saw a bit of embarrassed uncertainty in his son's face and didn't like it.

"Do you mean the space in the tunnels below the statue of Dr. King?"

Danny said that he did.

"No, I don't believe anyone ever played dodgeball in there, but it would be good for that, wouldn't it?"

"Yeah. My dad thinks that the Hub was a fallout shelter."

It was Yeager's turn to look uncertain, and for that Donovan was grateful.

"It would be good for that, too," Donovan said. "Was it?"

By no means stammering, but quite uncertain, Yeager said, "The Hub . . . yes, fallout shelter . . . so I understand. It *was* used for that, I believe. It was well before my time."

"Mine too, pretty much," Donovan said.

"Why are you interested in . . . oh, yes, of course, the poor man who was found dead—"

"Murdered," Donovan said.

"Yes, horrible! Mr.—"

"Paz," Donovan said. "It means 'peace.' He died in a fallout shelter."

Yeager said, "Why are you interested? I thought you don't catch murderers anymore."

"*I* don't. My *son* does, apparently."

Proudly, the boy said, "I'm helping Uncle Brian catch a murderer."

"And Uncle Brian would be . . . ?"

"Brian Moskowitz, *Lieutenant* Moskowitz, who replaced me as head of Special Investigations," Donovan said.

"Well, sure. Let me know what I can do for you there, too."

"We will," Donovan said.

"Thank you," Danny said cheerfully.

And if Yeager thought that he was about to escape, Donovan said, "I think that my son has a question about bricks, too."

13. "I ALWAYS KNEW ONE DAY YOU'D COME WALKING BACK THROUGH MY DOOR"

On their way back to the Dannymobile, they found Brian Moskowitz occupying a primary-color-splashed folding lawn chair, $5.95, such as the old women used to sit in and gossip along Upper Broadway. He was finishing a burrito and washing it down with a bottle of malta, a nonalcoholic malt beverage.

"I'm absorbing local culture while waiting for you," he said.

"I thought you didn't want us butting in on your case," Donovan said.

"I don't. I was getting into my car when I saw this beat cop drive up and make like he was going to ticket your van. Guess what, he was one of my old *friends*, that smart-assed cop who kept getting in our way when that guy was being eaten by crows in Central Park."

"Lewis was here?" Donovan said, a bit of joy on his cheeks.

Patrolman Lewis Rodriguez was Donovan's eldest son, the result of a relationship he had with a Cuban barmaid more than two decades earlier. That relationship ended about as badly as relationships could end without emergency rooms being involved, and Rosie Rodriguez moved to Union City, New Jersey, where she assiduously kept Donovan in the dark about the existence of his firstborn. He eventually found out, and the two were reunited during the Central Park crow buffet. Lewis inherited Donovan's famous old rent-controlled apartment on Riverside Drive after his dad and Marcie moved into the Greenwich Village townhouse that subsequently became an

102

amusement to Donovan's old friends.

Mosko said, "He's patrolling this stretch of Broadway now, and I can tell you he is becoming every bit as charming as you."

Donovan didn't stop beaming.

"Hiya, kid," Mosko said to Danny.

"Hi, Uncle Brian," the boy said.

Then, quickly and beaming with pride to match his dad's, Danny said, "I found out that what Mr. Franks said was true. The Hub used to be used as a fallout shelter!"

"Good work! Guess what I found out."

Mosko was addressing the boy, and Donovan said, "You can tell me too if you want."

"That's okay. We cool," Mosko said.

"What did you find?" Danny asked.

"Ask your dad if he remembers I said there were a lot of neatly arranged *National Geographic*s in Paz's apartment."

"I remember," Donovan grumbled.

"Ask him if he knows the word 'Chernobyl.' "

"Dad?"

"Where are we going with this?" Donovan asked.

Mosko looked at his old boss. "Where we are going—where Paz was going, at least in his reading interests—was Chernobyl. And Hiroshima. And Nagasaki, and Alamogordo, and Bikini Atoll, and Three Mile Island and—"

"Everywhere there was a nuclear blast, or one or another accident," Donovan said.

"You got it, Dad. He read up on the environmental effects of nuclear explosions, nuclear fallout . . . oh, and there were articles on strontium ninety, which I'm proud to say I Googled and—"

"It's a radioactive ingredient of the fallout that everyone was afraid would get into the milk supply," Donovan said.

"Yeah, and if you weren't so much older than me, you would

have had to Google it too."

"Paz was also obsessed with radiation at nuclear power plants and research facilities," Mosko said. "Such as this one."

He stomped the ground to make his point about the pioneering nuclear research done at Riverside by Samuel Franks and colleagues half a century earlier.

"Damn," Donovan said.

"He had the magazines neatly lined up in chronological order," Mosko said.

"And was considered creepy because he was always volunteering to do extra basement cleanup. But wait, Keogh said that the nuclear research was done in the second sub-basement of the physics building."

"Which is a National Historic Site."

"Not the Hub, except that it used to be a fallout shelter," Donovan said.

"There's a thread," Mosko said.

"Why was this plain-vanilla Latino janitor obsessing on nuclear bombs and fallout and poking around beneath an eminent research institution that did pioneering bomb research back when the Cold War was barely an ice cube?"

"And why did it get him killed?"

"Did it?" Donovan asked.

"Well, he had no woman problems, no drug problems, no beefs with neighbors that I can find," Mosko said.

"So it most likely was his atomic obsession that killed him."

Nodding, Mosko said, "My life is a lot more interesting than yours."

"Where the hell is Franks?" Donovan asked.

"I liked it when he asked about the Beast," Danny said.

"And who helped create a damned good beast of his own. Where is he? He said he was going to be at the faculty reception."

"Probably down in the National Historic Site building another bomb," Mosko said.

"McGowan is missing," Donovan said. "Franks was a no-show at the party he invited me to. This campus is getting on my nerves."

"Let's go see," Danny said, a bit too eagerly, and then a bit too rapidly wheeling his chair around so that he was hiding behind a wire mesh trash can.

Donovan saw Mary coming up then, chatting with her American cousin's firstborn, who was wearing a sweater and jeans and carrying two armloads of packages.

"*Oy vey,* more Donovans," Mosko said.

"Sorry, slugger," the Captain said to his youngest, "it's late and you're gonna have to go home for dinner."

"Dad, *please.* I won't get in the way."

"I know that."

"Uncle Brian will say that I'm being a help."

"You are. You're being a bigger help than your dad. But you won't be if you don't get a good dinner, and a good sleep."

"Can I come with you tomorrow?" the boy pleaded.

"If your dad says it's okay," Mosko said.

Donovan said that it was.

"'Tomorrow after school is Daniel's physical therapy day," Mary scolded.

"Do I have to go? It's boring."

Donovan hemmed a little, then hawed a bit, and finally said, "You'll have to ask your mom."

"Mom's *never there,*" Danny said.

The grown-ups exchanged looks.

"Try to track her down," Donovan said. "If anyone can do it, you can. Tell her I said it was okay for you to come help Uncle Brian after school tomorrow."

"Yeah!" the boy exclaimed.

Mary said, "Marcie is going to have your head."

"You mean the stuffed one on the wall?" Donovan asked.

When the Dannymobile was loaded with packages and Danny started off back down Broadway, Donovan gave Lewis a hug and said, "Thanks for not ticketing the van before."

"Mr. Wonderful here talked me into going easy on you."

"Make that *Lieutenant* Wonderful, kid," Mosko said. Then he clasped the young officer's hand and said, "I gotta go take care of something. You look after your old man now."

"Sure. See you, Lieutenant."

To Donovan, Mosko said, "I only gave you the news about Paz as a courtesy. You get your ass back into finding McGowan and leave me alone. If I need any help from a Donovan, I got me one."

"Awright. Get the fuck outta here."

When Mosko was back across the street and the lights were coming on the length of Broadway, the beer signs were on in the Rosa Blanca, Donovan said to Lewis, "You're off duty. Let me buy you a beer."

He hooked a thumb in the direction of the door to the bar.

"It's on me," Lewis said. "Actually, it's on the house tonight."

"What happened, did George get a personality transplant?"

Smiling wickedly, Lewis said, "George is off the night shift. The new woman is replacing him."

"Woman? A barmaid, in this joint?"

"She has lots of experience. Come on in. She wants to see you."

"Wants to see me?" Donovan asked, as he found himself with a hand on his back urging him through the door and inside.

He saw a barfull of old familiar faces smiling at him, smiling as if they were in possession of some great secret.

"*Again*," Lewis said, "she wants to see you *again*."

"Again?"

Donovan looked over his shoulder at his firstborn and then behind the bar and saw her, smiling. Her blond hair was still blond, her face round and cherubically sexy, and while he couldn't see it behind the bar, he was sure that her butt was still big, round, and beautiful even after twenty years.

"Rosie," he said, nearly a gasp.

Smiling the same smile as the crowd of old friends, Rosie Rodriguez, the love of Donovan's life way back before the years forced them, kicking and screaming, to grow up, and sent them in wrong directions. Rosie Rodriguez, Lewis's mother, put a hand on a hip and cocked it in the direction of the beer taps. "Bill Donovan," she said, spicing her words with an ironic grin and a really bad Karen Allen imitation, "I always knew one day you'd come walking back through my door."

"Welcome home, Dad," Lewis said as the bar cheered.

14. "WHAT YOU *DID* TO ME, TO MY LIFE"

Astonished and at first nearly speechless, Donovan walked to the end of the bar where the gate was. When it swung open she fell into his arms, and they kissed and hugged. They held each other tight, then he held her at arm's length for the expected inspection, and she did the same.

"You haven't changed," he said, smiling just enough to let her know that he meant it reasonably enough.

She was pretty much as he imagined on those long nights when Marcie was out being a lawyer and he felt lonely and needed something, or someone, warm to think about. A few years back Lewis had told him that she put on weight, but she had lost it. There were wrinkles in the expected places, but not so many, and the blond hair was enhanced, which was expected.

Most important, she was smiling. She said, "You haven't gotten older. You look just the same."

"Well, thank you for saying that."

"No, really. Is your hair the natural color?" She ruffled it and looked more closely. "It is. How could you do that to me, keep your natural color?"

"There's less of it now."

She made a point of looking at that, then said, "Yeah."

"Thanks for noticing."

"Hey, there's *more* of my butt," she said.

Donovan made an exaggerated point of looking at it. "Nice," he said.

"How old are you now?" she asked.

The smile drooped a bit. He said, "Do we have to go there?"

She nodded.

He sighed, then said, "Fifty-five."

"Oh my God. How old were you when we were together?"

"Thirty-five, *mas o menos*. And you?"

"Never ask a woman that question," she said.

"I guess we're not enemies anymore," he said.

"We were never enemies," she replied. "I just hated you, that's all."

"I'm relieved."

"Man, what you *did* to me, to my life! When you ran off with that black woman. Mary something."

"Marcie, and she's half white. And I've seen *Raiders of the Lost Ark* forty times, including the first time, when we saw it together. Now can we act like normal people and quote *Casablanca*? 'Of all the gin joints in all the towns in all the world . . .' works."

"I was *pregnant*," Rosie said.

"You might have *told* me," he replied. "It took me years to find out—on my own—that I had a son."

"Is she still with you?"

"Mas o menos," he replied. "More *menos* these days."

"Your marriage is winding down?"

"It's . . . ah . . . it's . . ."

"It's winding down," she said.

"I don't want to talk about it," Donovan replied.

"I hated you for a long time after you left me for her."

"And I hated you for a long time for not telling me about Lewis," Donovan said.

"I named him after your grandfather, didn't I?" she replied.

"I wondered why you picked that name," he said.

"If he turned out to be a girl I would have named him

Sharon, who lived next door, my friend, the ballerina. Remember her?"

Donovan nodded. "She had a nice butt, too."

"But he wasn't, and I named him after your grandfather. I liked your grandfather."

"Whatever else we did or didn't do, we made a pretty good kid," Donovan said. "He saved my life two or three years ago."

"I heard about that. That's when I decided we needed to reconnect. I realized that you weren't bulletproof after all. That's how you used to seem."

"You wanted to reconnect two or three years ago? What took you so long?"

"*My* marriage was winding down, but I had to lose the husband first," she said with a laugh. "And I had to lose weight."

Lewis came up then, and the three of them hugged, then she said, "Go down the bar and take your usual stool. I have to serve some of these bums."

Donovan did as he was told, but before he sat down in his customary spot just to the Broadway side of Jake, Donovan fished two fifties out of his wallet and waved them in the air and said, "All of 'em, Rosie—one last time."

It took her fifteen or twenty minutes to refresh everyone's drinks, then she came over to where Donovan sat flanked by Lewis and Jake.

"It's good to see you guys together again," Jake said.

"Time had to go by," she replied.

"What's happening with Union City?" Donovan asked. "Are you still living there?"

"I was until a week ago. My building is being torn down for condos."

Donovan shook his head. Developers destroying neighbor-hoods to make way for upper-income residences was one of his red-flag issues.

"Where are you living now?"

"In the city," she said coyly.

"Where in the city?" he asked.

"On Riverside Drive."

Donovan thought, had one of those lightbulb-over-the-head moments, then said, "You're in my old apartment."

"It's Lewis's apartment now," she said.

Lewis said, "Actually, I think his name is still on the lease. No, wait . . . it can't be, because it was rent controlled when he got it from his parents, right, Dad?"

Donovan smiled.

"Your father's name is on the lease then?" Lewis asked.

"The name on the lease is my grandfather's—Lewis."

Mother and son laughed.

Donovan hoisted his bottle of Bud and said, "To Lewis."

Jake raised his and toasted, "Twenty-nine missions!"

Rosie laughed, really laughed, and said, "God, I forgot about the twenty-nine missions!" She raised her glass.

"What happened to your walk-up?" Donovan asked her.

"My sister's son has it. You remember Camelia?"

Donovan remembered. "I remember her freaking out when she found the beer cans and box of moldy Wheat Thins under the bed."

"Wrong. It was *me* who freaked out," Rosie said. "You know, you and I made Lewis in your apartment. Possibly in the bed I'm sleeping in now. That was after the Wheat Thins were gone, though."

Lewis looked away.

Rosie said, "You have another kid now. Danny? He's okay . . . ?"

Donovan nodded, then added, "He's a great kid."

"A really great kid," Lewis said.

Donovan continued, "But both his legs are paralyzed. No one knows why."

"I'm sorry," Rosie said, reaching across the bar and touching Donovan's hand.

"I retired so I could spend all my time tracking down this scientist who might be able to help him. The guy used to work over there." Donovan hooked a thumb in the direction of the Riverside campus. "But I haven't been able to find him."

"You will," Rosie said.

"Danny's been coming along with me," Donovan said. "He's been helping me. Actually, lately he's been helping Mosko solve a murder."

"What's a 'Mosko'?"

"Brian Moskowitz. Replaced me as head of Special Investigations when I retired."

"Oh yeah, I heard about him. 'Mr. Wonderful.' "

"*Lieutenant* Wonderful," Lewis said.

"Who's the vic?"

"A nothing named Gregorio Paz," Donovan replied.

"From around here?" she asked.

"A block or two uptown. Near the Wendy's."

"Is he the guy whose body was found in the library across the street? Oh, wait . . . *you* found him."

"I'm lucky that way," Donovan said.

"There's so much of your life that I missed out on," Rosie said. "When I think of the things you and I could have done together . . ."

"This sort of talk will get us nowhere," Donovan said.

"You became famous. You became the most famous detective in America."

"The most famous detective in America couldn't figure out that his girlfriend was pregnant," Donovan said.

"You were on *Larry King*," she said.

"Once, and it was only because Mosko and I caught a terrorist. The moment passed. It's over. History. *Finito!*"

"Captain Donovan," she said with a sigh, touching her fingertips to his hand a second time.

15. You sit and stare at something long enough, it gets embarrassed and explains itself

"Let me see if I can get this straight," Mosko said.

"If you figure it out, explain it to me," Donovan replied.

"Before I came into your life your partner was Tom Jefferson, right?"

"Right."

"I remember him. He seemed okay."

"He was okay," Donovan agreed.

"The two of you worked out of the old West Side Major Crimes Unit on Broadway near Zabar's, correct?"

Donovan said that was correct.

"You were a lieutenant, he was a sergeant. It was your unit."

"Right-o," Donovan replied, taking the cup of coffee he just picked up at the bodega on 136th Street and stirring it with the ass end of a ballpoint pen. They were walking down Broadway toward the campus.

"When you made captain and got the citywide command—Special Investigations, which I so capably run these days—"

"Very capably."

"He made lieutenant and took charge of the West Side Major Crimes Unit."

"You got it," Donovan said.

"And now what?"

"The West Side Major Crimes Unit is no more and Jefferson is deputy chief of detectives, Manhattan North."

"Oh, okay. I'm catching on. Now I remember reading about

his promotion. We've gotten way ahead of ourselves. Tell me—way back when, Marcie and Jefferson were an item?"

"Christ no," Donovan said, crossing himself. "They hated each other, in a friendly kind of way. See, Jefferson was very black and by that I mean a black chauvinist, who didn't like the fact that Marcie was half white. This was at the tail end of the Black Power movement. He called her 'high yellow,' which is an old-time black slur against what they used to call 'mulattos,' which nowadays in this enlightened cultural atmosphere we call 'multi-racial.' "

"Cultural history kinda makes you dizzy, doesn't it?" Mosko said.

Nodding, Donovan said, "Jefferson also thought that she was a princess—"

"I'm shocked."

"Shocked," Donovan said. "And *she* thought that he was low class, the Brooks Brothers suits notwithstanding."

"But *you* and Marcie were an item," Mosko said.

"Yeah, going back twenty-five years when I was teaching a seminar at Columbia Law and she was a student. We had an affair, she gave up her plans to become a lawyer, she followed me into the NYPD, and before too long she was away from me doing undercover in Harlem and fighting with Jefferson. Sooo . . . we broke up and I fell in love with a Cuban barmaid—"

"Rosalie Rodriguez."

"Who was working at this dive on Broadway down in the eighties, right by the unit."

"When you were drunk all the time," Mosko said.

"I wasn't drunk *all* the time. Occasionally I took a shower. Anyway," Donovan continued, "I fell really hard for Rosie as she did for me, and we were living at my place and were going to get married and have children, except that she didn't want to wait for the marriage part, and"—Donovan waved an index

115

finger in the air, making a circular movement, as if stirring soup—"and Marcie came to work undercover for me and was gut-shot and nearly killed. I felt it was my fault and, I don't know, before too long Rosie was out and Marcie was in again. I kinda lose track of the sequence."

"*You're* confused?" Mosko said.

"And the rest you know, except that after Marcie and I had Danny, and he turned seven or eight, I began spending more and more time trying to find a cure for him, and less and less time with Marcie. She went back to Columbia Law to pick up where she left off before I got into her life and messed up her plans."

"That's when you knew it was over," Mosko said.

"I knew it was *winding down*," Donovan replied. "What can I tell you, man . . . a relationship with a woman is something I could never get straight."

"Who *can?*"

"You're not doing a bad job," Donovan said.

"I'm not inclined to question everything like you do."

"So now, here I am, marriage winding down, Rosie suddenly sprung on me out of nowhere, looking good and she's been working on it for two or three years building up to seeing me again, which certainly shows *something,* as does the fact that Lewis and her have been in cahoots."

"This isn't just a game that's being played on you, *amigo,*" Mosko said. "This is the fucking World Cup."

"I know, but it's nice to be wanted," Donovan said. "It's nice to feel a little warmth."

"Warm the bench for a while."

"I intend to do just that. I've had enough *woman* to last me a long time."

"Like for a decade or two. Hold on while I run inside for a donut."

Donovan stood on the sunrise sidewalk, watching the long shadows growing shorter across the beloved Broadway that he had seen far too little of in recent years.

The facade of the Rosa Blanca stood silent and sad with no lights on, and instead the ghost in the bricks of its yesteryears as a garage hung over the concrete. Burrito paper and crumpled burger wrappers from the Wendy's littered its feet.

Mosko came out of the store munching a cinnamon cruller.

"That's gonna kill you," Donovan said.

"Not as fast as women are going to kill you. Let's cross the street and go onto the campus. Keogh arranged to let us into the physics building."

Keogh had a ring of keys that hung from his belt and clattered against his thigh as he trudged along. He had met them under the King statue and led the way across the campus to the physics building, which looked to Donovan old enough for its stones to have been carved from the trunk of the apple tree from which Newton's apple fell. But it was built of stone blocks that appeared as old and as immovable as Manhattan itself, and perfectly able to hide secrets.

"I hope you guys know what you're looking for," said the retired cop, pulling a thick slab of key out of the pack and slipping it into an equally formidable lock.

"I don't care if we know what we're looking for as long as we find it," Mosko said.

"Huh?" Keogh mumbled.

"When you're up against a case that seems to make no sense—"

Donovan cut in and added, "Try to beat it at its own game."

Keogh didn't say "huh?" again, but he *looked* "huh."

Mosko said, "Sometimes you just have to sit down next to a problem and wait until it offers its own solution."

To his old partner, Donovan said, "I'm proud of you, my son," beaming that he had so successfully passed to another generation his "method detecting" approach to crime solving. You sit and stare at something long enough, it gets embarrassed and explains itself.

Method detecting worked wonders on difficult cases. It also worked wonders on overtime pay.

Keogh appeared undecided whether he was being made fun of, and opted for caution. He said, "I think I'll leave you guys on your own and go grab some breakfast."

"Thanks for letting us in," Mosko said.

"Call me on the cell if you need anything."

"Will do," Donovan replied.

"Try not to break stuff," the man said and was gone, huffing as he bore his oversized belly away from the building and toward Broadway.

"Well, that gets rid of *him*," Mosko said.

"He isn't being very helpful, is he?" Donovan said.

"He's come up with a few things. Still, I'd just as soon he not hang around."

"Throughout his career as a cop, most of his superior officers felt that way," Donovan said. "It's not that he was a bad cop. He got on people's nerves just standing around, and so you tended to pat him on the back, thank him for showing up, and then ask him to go stand around somewhere else. He drew his paycheck for as long as he needed to get his pension."

"Lots of guys do it," Mosko said.

The two men found the bank of four elevators, summoned one, and rode the half-century-old clattering box down two levels into Manhattan bedrock. Once again, Donovan felt himself approaching the core of the earth.

When the door clanked open again, they were staring at yet another dark corridor, this one painted white but with the lights off. It was lit only by the light from the elevator car and from a sort of yellow emanation from down to the right.

Donovan flicked on his Maglite long enough for Mosko to find the switch that put on the hall lights—fluorescent and hung from rods, two feet below the high ceiling of the hall and let them see the bronze plaque on the wall across from the elevator. It read:

Site of basic atomic research that was a vital part of the Allied construction of the Atomic Bomb dropped on Hiroshima, August 6, 1945, resulting in the surrender of the Japanese Empire, ending World War II. This was the laboratory of Nobel Prize–winning physicist Samuel Franks, who conducted the first uranium isotope separation. Designated a National Historic Site August 6, 1955.

Mosko said, "Kablam!"

Donovan said, "Twenty-nine missions," and saluted.

"So this is where the atomic age was born," Mosko said.

"Here, and Columbia, and the University of Chicago, and a few other places," Donovan said.

"All the shit that went down here was well known."

"Excruciatingly," Donovan said.

"Dozens of books written about it."

"Hundreds."

"What did Gregorio Paz think he was going to find?" Mosko asked.

Donovan offered to the chasm a quizzical look. "Nobels were awarded for this research. Pulitzers were awarded for writing about it. This is not to mention thousands of doctoral dissertations, some of which Danny and I desecrated the other day. Digging around down here is like looking for fossilized mammoths in Siberia. Been there, dug that."

119

"The environmental effects of atomic research—" Mosko offered.

"Been there . . ."

"Right, and there are more recent things to look into."

"The mutant rats of Chernobyl," Donovan said.

"I don't know what the hell I'm looking for," Mosko said.

"Remember what I taught you. The instant you give up looking, that's the second you find it," Donovan said.

"So when are Rosie and you getting together again?" Mosko asked.

Donovan told him to fuck himself.

There was a metallic noise, a ringing noise, the sound of something metal being dropped. It came from down the hall from whence also came the yellow light they saw when first exiting the elevator.

In one uniform motion, Donovan and Mosko pulled their handguns and aimed them down the hall, Mosko dropping to the low position.

16. "ONE FLEW EAST, ONE FLEW WEST . . ."

The light came from beyond two heavy metal doors, lead bordered with something else, that hung in the stale air like the bay doors to submarine bases. Or such things as Donovan imagined them without knowing if they existed at all.

"It's six in the morning," Mosko said.

"Who's gonna be working down there?" Donovan asked.

"It's not a *working* lab, even. It's a goddam museum. And the janitorial staff doesn't come in until seven."

"After you," Donovan said.

"Oh, thanks."

"You're the boss man now."

"Why *are* you here anyway?" Mosko said.

"I have to give Patrick McGowan a rest for a while," Donovan said. "I'm not giving up, just taking a break to—"

"To make my life miserable."

"To see if I get any new ideas. Making your life miserable is a value-added."

"Let's go," Mosko said, and led the way.

They crept down the hall, looking and listening, feeling a tingle of excitement concurrent with the fear that they were about to make horrible fools of themselves. When they got to the door, Mosko asserted the lead, waving Donovan patronizingly, he thought, to stay back. So that's what the captain did and, a few seconds later, Mosko said, "Oh, balls."

Donovan put away his gun and looked over his old partner's shoulder.

There was Samuel Franks, a white apron pulled over his dark suit, staring down at the floor.

"I seem to have had an accident," he said, having scantly noticed the appearance of the two detectives.

On the floor were several pieces of a metal rod which, not too long before, had fit together quite well, it appeared. Franks looked embarrassed by his part in their disassembly.

"I'm not as adept as I used to be," he added.

"Neither is he," Mosko said, indicating Donovan, who was already on his knees retrieving the pieces.

"What is this?" Donovan asked.

"Oh, it's one of my old tie rods. It holds together several components of the aligner."

"What's that do?" Mosko asked.

"It aligns," Donovan said, getting to his feet.

"Aligns what?"

Franks showed them a refrigerator-sized mass of rods, plates, geared wheels, and clamps. "This," he said.

"Do we need to know what that is?" Donovan asked.

"Not unless you're studying the history of twentieth-century nuclear research," Franks said. "Are you?"

"Tomorrow," Mosko replied.

"Well then, I suggest you concern yourself with why you *are* here, which is?"

"To ask what you're doing in this museum at six in the morning," Mosko said.

"Thinking," Franks said.

He took the pieces from Donovan and, after a moment's worth of listless attempts to put them back together, placed them on one of the plates of the aligner. Then he took off the apron.

"Thinking about what?" Donovan asked.

The old man sighed, and said, "Oh, I'm not sure. What we did here so long ago. What happened. What didn't happen. Why I can't seem to put that tie rod back together."

"May I?" Donovan asked.

He picked up the pieces and twisted them around, trying several combinations, before having them snatched away by Moskowitz.

"Let the guy who works on his own car handle this," he said, and with several deft motions the gadget was back together.

Franks smiled, took it from Mosko, then put it back down.

"We're wondering if the research conducted here has something to do with the murder of Gregorio Paz," Mosko said.

"That would be the poor man whose body was found in the tunnel by my library?" Franks asked.

Donovan told him that he was correct.

"I can't imagine a connection. What do you think it might be?"

"He was obsessed with nuclear research, especially the environmental consequences," Donovan said.

"What form did that obsession take?" Franks asked.

"Reading popular accounts," Donovan said. "And volunteering to do a lot of cleaning up of basements around here that have something or other to do with nuclear research, or fallout shelters, or something."

"I'm afraid I can't help. Perhaps he was simply interested in the subject. Some men collect coins, others—"

"Prowl the corridors where the nuclear age was launched," Donovan said.

"It's coming back, you know, the nuclear age," Franks said. "What with the price of gasoline these days, everyone's rethinking nuclear power. I think that's a good thing. We can't be held hostage to the Arabs forever."

"Can you think of *any* connection between Paz's work and yours?" Mosko asked.

The old man thought for a moment, then said, "Well, I suppose there was the reception."

"What reception?" Mosko asked. "The one yesterday?"

"Oh no," Franks said. "And Captain, I believed I promised to meet you there, didn't I?"

Donovan nodded. "It's okay."

"I took a nap and slept right through it," Franks said. "I need a nap now and then. I must be getting old."

"Untrue," Donovan said.

"That's what Nurse Ratched would say, were she here."

Smiling, Donovan asked, "Did you read the book or see the play, or the movie?"

"What?" Mosko asked.

"*One Flew over the Cuckoo's Nest,*" Donovan said. "Nurse Ratched was the evil voice of silence and conformity."

"Who gave Jack Nicholson a lobotomy, I remember it now. My Uncle Stanley sometimes could use one of those."

"I read the book *and* saw the play and movie," Franks said. "Wonderful, wonderful. Anyway, I got rid of her today by claiming to have lost my asthma inhaler and sending her off to look for it. She thought, 'The old man is alone in the basement with his memories, how much trouble can he get into?' "

"What are 'they' afraid you will say?" Donovan asked.

"So afraid that they give you a PhD nurse," Mosko added.

"Who knows so little about medicine that she hasn't figured out that I don't have asthma, I only fake pulmonary symptoms so that I can 'lose' my inhaler and send her off on missions looking for it."

"What secrets can you tell that haven't been told?" Donovan asked.

Franks said, "For the life of me I don't know. Everything in this room . . . in the bomb program . . . has been very well described. 'They'—"

"Who?" Mosko asked.

Franks picked up a piece of pipe and twisted it about. He said, "I don't know that either. The university—in the person of Provost Yeager—said *they* wanted to be sure I lived to be one hundred. They say they're afraid I would fall. There are, you know, two hundred and twenty-four steps that one must negotiate to get up to the administration building. I once calculated that I had walked up and down more than a quarter million of them in my life here. I *did* fall once, at Faculty Club, but the culprit was gin and I don't consider it a chronic problem. I suppose I *might* fall seriously one day, so in a way it's not so bad to have her around. At any rate, she's a harmless nuisance. And we've all lived with those."

He handed the piece of pipe to Mosko.

"I've lived with more than a quarter million of them," Donovan said.

"All of them cousins from Ireland," Mosko added.

"When I get too chatty she whisks me away. I suppose they think I'm losing it. In fact, I'm sure they do. Maybe I am. After all, I couldn't put that device back together." He pointed at it.

"Neither could I," Donovan said.

Apparently losing interest in an old man and his problems, Mosko said, "You mentioned a reception. What reception?"

"Why, the one we held a few years ago for the anniversary. Mr. Paz cleaned up the Hub before the reception. He did a wonderful job, too. It sparkled."

"The anniversary of what?" Donovan asked.

"The sixtieth anniversary of our successful isotope separation," Franks said proudly. "It was a necessary step to our achieving fission."

"Where was the reception?" Mosko asked.

"In the Hub, of course. That was my idea, I'm afraid. You know, have the anniversary of our isotope separation in the old fallout shelter. I thought it was amusing."

"Sounds like a laugh riot to me," Mosko said.

"Where *did* you do the isotope separation?" Donovan asked, "Here?"

He went to pick up the tie rod. Then he thought better of it, and instead rubbed his palm against his pants.

Before he could get his answer, there was a clatter of feet on cold floor and the appearance of Marion Riggs, RN, PhD.

"Professor!" she said.

"*Oy*," he uttered.

"What have you been doing?" she asked, her voice accompanied by a forced laugh.

With a forced laugh of his own, Donovan said, "Ah, just entertaining two flatfeet with his tales of the Cold War. And you?"

She said, "Ah . . . I . . . didn't expect anyone to be here with Professor Franks."

"Cops," Mosko said. "They turn up at the least convenient times."

"Did you find my inhaler?" Franks asked.

"Oh, the inhaler. Yes. You left it on the coffee table. Here."

She handed him the palm-sized tube. He put it to his lips and gave himself a puff of harmless topical steroid, then offered Donovan a hidden smile.

Nurse Riggs didn't quite see the smile, but she must have suspected something, for she turned to give the old man a closer look. In that instant, Mosko tapped her on the arm and said, "Hey yo, whaddya make of this?"

He handed her the piece of pipe he got from Franks. Then he continued, "You're a medical person. My friend here"—he indicated Donovan—"thinks it comes from an iron lung. I got a bet with him. Whaddya say?"

Caught off guard twice now—by smile and pipe—Nurse Riggs was flustered enough to look at the pipe, turning it over and over as if what she just heard was a serious question. Then she said, "It's . . . part of this machine." And she nodded at the whatever-it-was before handing back the pipe.

Mosko looked at Donovan and said, "You owe me ten bucks. Fork it over."

Donovan pulled out his wallet, peeked inside, then said, "You got change for a fifty?"

"Later," Mosko said, and away went the wallet.

The nurse said, "Professor, you really shouldn't be alone. What if you had an accident? What if you fell?"

"I had two of New York's finest to rescue me," Franks said.

"We should go now. Are you finished here?"

"Doctor Riggs, I was finished here in 1947."

"Then why do you keep coming back?" Mosko asked.

"I honestly don't know. All the stories have been told."

"Have they?" Donovan asked.

"I assure you," Franks said, offering a wink just before he allowed himself to be led off.

They two detectives stood in silence watching. Then when they were alone, Mosko said, "What do you want to do now, split an atom?"

As if there might be an explosion inside it, he held the piece of pipe up to glint in the light.

"Prints?" Donovan asked.

"I see at least two doozies," Mosko replied.

"I want to know who this fucking bitch is," Donovan replied.

17. "KICK THE SHIT OUT OF HIM AND CUFF HIM TO THE RADIATOR IN MY OFFICE"

"This is like your apartment, Dad," Danny said.

He had maneuvered the Beast over to one of two huge living room windows and was looking out over the Hudson River, which at that spot on the Manhattan shoreline rolled down under the George Washington Bridge. That was how the rest of America drove north to Boston, skimming the concrete jungle gym of Manhattan.

"Where do you live?" asked Provost Yeager.

"Riverside and Eighty-ninth—no, sorry, I meant in the Village. I *used* to live on Riverside."

Yeager asked where in the Village, and Donovan related that he lived on Stuyvesant Street near the historic and currently trendy Gansevoort Meat Market.

"However did you get an apartment *there?*" Yeager asked. "It's very hot."

"The slabs of beef are gone, and no more loading docks full of chicken livers. But Stella McCartney has a boutique there, so all is not lost . . . the invasion of sidewalk café slaughter has begun. Do you know that it's possible to pay twenty-five dollars for a cheeseburger?"

"Dad's apartment is bigger than this," Danny said.

"This one is a *nice* apartment," Donovan said. "How many bedrooms?"

Yeager said that there were three.

"My dad's apartment has three bedrooms too. My brother

128

Lewis lives there. And I have a room there too. I lived in it before we moved to the Village."

"Lewis is grown," Donovan said. "He's from a previous relationship. Tell me whatever you can about McGowan's having lived here."

The Captain was relieved when his change of conversation worked.

"As I told you before, there's not much to tell," Yeager said. "We placed him here as an inducement to lure him away from Stanford. He lived here. Then he disappeared, and he didn't live here anymore. I took the apartment."

"What kind of time frame are we talking about?" Donovan asked. "When did he disappear and when did you take over the apartment?"

Yeager thought for a few seconds, then said, "McGowan disappeared . . . his colleagues began to notice in the middle of the month when he stopped going to meetings. He was never very good at that, and it took us a while to realize there was something wrong. So when it was clear he was gone without a trace—"

"When was that?"

"Oh, around the middle of July. Early August. We began making calls—everywhere, like you're doing now. But as you doubtless know, McGowan has no family. No siblings or other relatives that we know of. His parents died young—his father in his sixties of Parkinson's. We always thought that was a driving force in McGowan's career."

Donovan nodded. Then he asked, "And you took over the apartment when?"

"Right after Labor Day," Yeager said.

"That was fast."

"He was gone, and it's the Gold Coast. This apartment and the others like it are worth a fortune."

"I thought you need to keep these for luring hotshot faculty away from Stanford," Donovan said.

"We do. Including me."

Yeager offered a slight self-satisfied smile.

"You were thinking of leaving?"

"Everyone does, from time to time. But in the end I stayed. Look, I know you came here to poke around and you're welcome to, but I want to give you this first."

He handed over a large envelope, of the sort that organizations use to route correspondence—or did until email took over office communications. It had holes in it and lines on which to put the routing list.

"I thought you didn't have anything," Donovan said.

"That envelope has holes in it," Danny said.

"It was on the top shelf of the pantry under a can of paint," Yeager said.

"You never erase *all* traces of old tenants," Donovan said.

He took out a handful of papers. Most were pay stubs bearing the Riverside Drive address. There also were menus from two Chinese restaurants, three parking tickets, and a slip of paper on which was written a phone number in area code 718.

"What's this number?" Donovan asked.

Yeager peered at it. "That area code is the Bronx and Queens, isn't it?" he replied.

"And Brooklyn and Staten Island," Donovan said.

"I don't spend much time in either. Mainly to drive through."

Donovan took out his cell phone and dialed the number. Then he put the phone back in his pocket. "Albert Einstein College of Medicine," he said.

"Did he talk to Einstein?" Yeager said. "I guess it's possible. He didn't go, though."

"Maybe they offered him an apartment on Mosholu Parkway," Donovan said.

"That's not exactly the Gold Coast," Yeager added. "Not that I've ever been there."

"The parking tickets are all on Morris Park Avenue. Near the medical center," Donovan said.

"You'd have to ask Einstein. All I can say is that if he thought of moving to Einstein, this is the first I've heard of it."

Donovan thought for a moment, then dropped the papers back into the envelope and slid it into his shoulder bag. He said, "I'll take you up on looking around the apartment, but first . . . tell me why Samuel Franks has a babysitter."

"A babysitter?" Yeager laughed. "She's his *nurse*."

"A PhD nurse? Will you warrant a PhD nurse when you're old enough to need one?"

"If I win a Nobel Prize and have a history of falling. A nasty fall can be the beginning of the end for a man of his years. My father died after a fall. Is *your* father still with us?"

Donovan shook his head.

"If you don't mind my asking, how did he die?"

"He was shot by a junkie," Donovan said.

Yeager had on his face the look of a man who had finally realized what bad a line of conversation he had chosen.

"He was a cop too," Donovan added.

"I am *so* sorry. I was trying to make a point."

"So was the junkie. Why does Franks' nurse feel the need to keep him quiet?"

"Is that what she's doing?" Yeager asked. "I imagine she's trying to prevent him from taxing himself."

Donovan *mmmfed*.

"*Why* are you interested in Professor Franks's medical issues?"

"Franks knew McGowan. He knew Paz."

"The janitor who was killed," Yeager said.

"All three," Donovan added.

"Are you saying there's a connection between Professor Franks, Patrick McGowan, and that man Paz?"

"What do *you* think?"

"I think . . . I think I don't see any similarities," a clearly unsettled provost replied.

"One was murdered. One disappeared under mysterious circumstances. One is being kept quiet," Donovan said. "May I look at the rest of your apartment now?"

"Can I come with you?" Danny asked.

"Always," Donovan said. And to Yeager he added, "We can find our way around."

" 'The time has come,' the walrus said," Donovan intoned, " 'to speak of many things.' "

"Huh?" Rosie replied.

"Lewis Carroll, *Through the Looking-Glass, and What Alice Found There*," Donovan said.

"I thought that was a Jefferson Airplane song," she said, washing a glass and putting it upside down on the bar.

"It was that, too."

"Do you want another beer?" she asked.

"I've had two. That's my limit these days."

"Three," she said. "You had three."

Donovan raised himself to full height, stretched to look over the bar, and said, "Your butt really *is* still pretty nice." So was the rest of her, even given the years, and Donovan was unable to hide his appreciation of the fact.

"I want to talk," Donovan said.

"I hear you do too much of that," she replied. "I don't think you're having enough fun."

"Why are you here? Why are you *really* here?"

He felt he could talk. The bar was empty. It was four-fifteen in the morning and they were alone.

"This is my world," she replied.

"Your world was in Union City."

"Before that, it was on Broadway. Your world was on Broadway too. Back then, long ago, when we were young—"

"And bulletproof," he added.

She sang a few words of "On Broadway."

Then she said, "We were happy then, you and I, and then you screwed me and nothing was the same again."

"How many times are we going to go over that?" he asked.

"Until I get it out of my system," Rosie said.

He sighed and said, "Back then I was afraid of getting married and settling down."

"Nobody asked you to get married."

"Having a kid is the same thing," he insisted. "I was a drunk and a reckless drunk."

"You were *fun*," she said. "You're not fun anymore. How long has it been since you laughed. Fall-down, rolling on the floor, stupid laugh. How long?"

"I would have wrecked your life."

"That's what you did anyway," she said.

Donovan replied, imitating Harrison Ford, "I did what I did. You don't have to be happy about it."

He wondered why it was that, in times of stress, so many people relied on words from the movies.

"I want to ask you, why Marcie? What did you see in her? What the fuck made her better than me? Was she better in bed? I doubt it, because she probably is afraid to get dirty. Do you remember how good we were in bed? We could be again. Was it her *sophistication?* Was it the hole she got in her belly when she was shot? You blamed yourself for that, even though it was bullshit. Was it guilt that made you leave me for her?"

Donovan looked at his beer bottle, trying to use it as a prism

133

through which to glare at the woman who once held his life in her hands.

"I . . . don't . . . want . . . to . . . do . . . this," he said, growling the words.

"Fuck what *you* want," she said. "I'm not done with you. Did you think that her wound was sexy? You must have, because it sure wasn't her *tits!* Was it because she's black? Did that turn you on? She can't have been a better fuck than me. Remember that time we fucked in the basement of Riley's and knocked over the beer kegs and one exploded. Tell me what it was about her. I know . . . it was her *money!*"

Sucking his breath in loud, like steam from a street vent at four in the morning, he slammed the bottle down on the bar hard enough to dent it. It shattered and, instantly, her lusty babe resolve temporarily AWOL, she jumped back, looking frightened.

He climbed over the bar—not quite jumping it as in the old days—but moving with ease, driven by anger and memories and her invitation to sex. She had her back to the backbar, tense with fear, and the bottles jingled.

Donovan grabbed her by the neck and by the shoulders, and then by the waist, and just as her fear crested, he jammed her against him, then with his body pressed her against the backbar. With his tongue he forced her lips open. She whimpered and submitted, and clutched him too, and then yanked his shirt open and the buttons went flying. So did the bottles, and he pulled her down to the floor.

Donovan slipped a hand down inside her jeans and grabbed her butt. But after a long moment, he let it go and pulled the hand out and eased his mouth back from hers. She whimpered again, and this time it was loud and with a pleading. He rolled away from her, sighing "No."

And she said "No" too, but it was in exasperation and anger.

He said "No" again and she gasped "Yes" and he said "Not *yet*," and then there was the sound of the cavalry charging over the hill, the door opening.

And a Brooklyn accent called out, "Hey yo."

"*Jee*sus!" she said, and rolled onto her back.

"Shit," Donovan said.

"You fuck! You incredible fuck!"

"Not *now*," he said again. "Too soon."

"You *fuck!* You're doing it to me *again!* You're rejecting me *again!*"

"I hear voices," Mosko said.

Donovan climbed to his feet, feeling the beginnings of pains in his elbows and knees from where he climbed over the bar. He tried to close his shirt, but without buttons it was hopeless. He tried to adjust his pants front, but that was hopeless too.

"Hi," he said sheepishly.

"You *fuck!*" she shrieked, still on the floor behind the bar, startling the lieutenant.

"I walked in on a party, didn't I?" he said after a moment.

"We were cleaning up," Donovan said.

"I see," Mosko replied. Then he added, "Look, this can keep until morning."

"It *is* morning," Donovan said.

The clock on the wall read five, and out on Broadway the City That Never Sleeps slumbered a bit, with only a far-off garbage truck and the rumble of the No. 1 local beneath their feet breaking the silence.

Rosie got to her feet then and tugged her jeans up. "Who the fuck are *you?*" she asked.

"This is Brian," Donovan said.

"Yeah, Lieutenant Wonderful. I heard all about you."

She bent and picked up a bottle of bourbon, twisted off the

cap, and took a slug. Then she held it out to Mosko and said, "Here."

"I gotta drive."

Then she offered it to Donovan and said, "Here, *asshole.*"

"I just love these family reunions," Mosko said.

"Me too," she said.

"I heard stories about how he used to be," Mosko said. "It looks like he's time-traveled back there."

"He's not there yet. I was working on it, I finally yanked him away from the glacier that cold bitch stranded him on, I had my hands on him, and then you came charging in. You're a fuck too. Go ahead, arrest me."

She took another shot.

Now that the front of his pants had settled down, Donovan walked around the bar, not climbing it this time, and asked "Why did you drive all the way here from the unit?"

He was aware of having said "unit," the old West Side Major Crimes Unit, and not One Police Plaza, the shiny highrise shrine to twenty-first-century crime fighting.

"News, bro'."

"That couldn't keep 'til normal business hours?"

"What was it this fuck used to say?" she asked. "Oh yeah, 'kick the shit out of him and cuff him to the radiator in my office.' "

Donovan couldn't help smiling. He was beginning to remember her better. Those were good times, some of them anyway, and he *did* roll on the floor laughing now and again.

And there *was* an exploding beer keg. Well, it hit the floor and popped its stopper.

To Mosko she said, "Does he even *have* a radiator in his Greenwich Village *townhouse?* Or is it all climate-controlled?"

"Lemme alone," Donovan snarled back.

"I'll leave you alone. I'll leave you forever alone."

And she began cleaning up the mess they made.

Mosko took a barstool—Jake's, as it turned out.

"Let me hear it," Donovan said, standing in front of him.

"Remember those prints on the piece of pipe? Remember them?"

"It was less then twenty-four hours ago. My short-term memory still can handle it."

"You can't remember how in love we were," Rosie called out, while sticking a bottle of cheap bourbon back on the shelf.

"Nurse Ratched isn't what she seems," Mosko said.

"She's a bitch who won't let a wise old man talk," Donovan said.

"What she *is*, is someone who works for a rent-a-nurse outfit, but she's also a PI."

"A private investigator."

"She has a carry permit," Mosko continued. "That's how her prints came up on the computer. She lugs around a nine millimeter automatic."

"Florence Nightingale with a firearm," Donovan said.

"She's a bodyguard—takes care of celebrities—rappers and that ilk—who in the course of their usual sinning may have need of medical attention."

"*He's* gonna need medical attention because I'm gonna fucking kill him," Rosie said.

She waved a bottle of sangria at Donovan.

"I want you to leave me alone," Donovan said over his shoulder.

To Mosko he asked, "What's the PhD for?"

"She ain't got one. It's phony. This house of higher learning across the street apparently never checked her credentials."

"Or didn't care," Donovan said lightly, although it was hardly that.

"Maybe they wanted her to sound legit," Mosko said.

137

Donovan nodded, and replied, "If the provost says you're a PhD, you're a PhD."

Mosko inhaled a great burst of some booze-laced air, and puffed himself up in the way that the Captain knew meant that he was working himself up for a pronouncement.

"Out with it," Donovan said.

"Guess who her boss at the PI firm is."

The Captain sucked in some air of his own, then said, "No. Not him."

"Him. All three hundred pounds of him."

"*Keogh?* Thomas J. Keogh. The guy I said was a useless bum."

"He's still a bum," Mosko said. "Only he's a smart and con-nected bum."

"*You're* the biggest bum," Rosie said.

Donovan turned toward her and snapped, "I want you out of my life again. I want you out of my apartment."

She gave him the finger, and he turned his attention back to his old partner.

"So Nurse Ratched is really a private eye and armed bodyguard who Riverside University is paying to keep their No-bel Prize–winning physicist who helped build the atomic bomb from shooting his mouth off," Donovan said.

"What the *fuck* are they doing over there?" Mosko asked, ad-dressing the smell of booze in the air.

"And what does it have to do with the disappearance of Patrick McGowan and the murder of Gregorio Paz?" Donovan asked the same night air.

"If it has anything to do with them," Mosko said.

"Oh, you think all this is coincidental?"

"What I think I need is a little sleep."

"Me too," Donovan said.

Mosko started toward the door, hesitated, turned back in the direction of his old boss, then at the door again, and then at

Donovan again.

"What?" the Captain asked.

"I was thinking. You know, you don't seem to be doing so good on finding McGowan, and the way things look around here you seem to be drifting back to the old days. I was wondering if maybe we could sort of get the old days back."

Donovan's eyes widened.

"I mean, you know, when we used to do things together, hang together, shoot some pool, watch the ball game on TV. Andy Pettit is back in a Yanks uniform this year. And maybe if you wouldn't mind hanging around the case and keeping me company," Mosko said, looking up at the ceiling and then back down. "I mean, I'm the boss this time, but you will respect that, and *you* can be the muscle for a while. You didn't throw such a bad punch on that guy in Brighton Beach, and from what I see you been kinda athletic in this dive tonight."

He looked at Rosie, who gave him the finger again.

"I mean, I'm running the unit now, and it's lonely at the top." He also appeared to enjoy having used the word "unit."

"Sure," Donovan said. "But only until this case is over and only if Danny comes with me."

"Sure," Mosko said with a big smile. "I'll be the brains, you be the muscle, Danny can be the wheels."

"Danny and I are a team now, and I guess we can take time out from finding McGowan to helping you find a killer."

"Out-fucking-standing," Mosko said, grabbing his old boss and friend's hand and pumping it.

Donovan yawned and said, "I need to sleep."

Mosko said, "I'll drop you off."

"You can drop him in the river," Rosie said, her hands on her hips.

Donovan looked sharply at her, but only for a moment, and then he looked sadly at her, and he turned to the door and on the way out he called over his shoulder and he said, "I want you out of my life again. I want you out of my apartment."

18. You can take the boy off Broadway, but you can't take Broadway out of the boy

"I want you out of my house," Marcie said.

"This has been *some* night," said her husband of record.

He stared at his cup of coffee. It might have stared back. He couldn't be sure. *Everything* seemed to be keenly observing his behavior.

Marcie had been doggedly cataloging his sins for nearly an hour.

"You have been *miserable* lately. You have treated *me* miserably."

"I'm surprised you've had time to notice," he said.

"Look, William. I wanted to be a lawyer when we met. But you hijacked my life for what was it, twenty years?"

"Nobody forced you to give up Columbia Law and become a cop."

"I was in love with you," she said.

"Maybe. But you were also bored with being a good little rich girl, and you wanted excitement. You got yourself a lover who had never been within the *shadow* of a prep school, and that wasn't jollies enough so you became a cop and went into the 'hood and you—"

He stopped abruptly, jammed on the hand brake, and the brakes squealed.

"What did you just *not* say?" Marcie asked.

"Nothing," he replied.

"What did you just not say?"

What Donovan had just not said was this: *You went into the 'hood with your privileged background and your stupid dreams of valorous cops and you gunned down two unarmed teenagers, albeit drug dealers, forcing the NYPD and in particular your future husband to cover up for you. You were the rich daughter of a state supreme court justice and a media mogul and you wouldn't have lasted an hour in prison, black belt or no. You broke up the long-running friendship of Bill Donovan and Tom Jefferson, made the young and innocent Brian Moskowitz complicit in manslaughter, and I never told you about it because I'm fucking old-fashioned and I believe in protecting people from monsters, if possible without their ever knowing there are monsters out there. And you repaid me by continuing to be a princess, dragging my son and me into a $5.5-million-dollar house that I hate, in a trendy neighborhood that I despise, and if that sounds like bullshit, a captain's pension ain't bad and now you are never home and damn, I want my old apartment and my good and forever friends back.*

Resolute to protect her from *that* nugget of information too, Donovan said, "I wasn't going to say anything."

"You were about to say something. You stopped."

"Something got stuck in my throat," he said.

To illustrate, he coughed into his coffee cup. But that only sent a spray of coffee onto his nose. That made him feel ridiculous on top of angry and tired. He wiped his nose on his sleeve. He had given up any shard of making an impression.

"You *tell me* what you were going to say," Marcie snapped, poking him on the chest with the tip of a finger.

That was, of course, enough to do it.

Donovan jumped up, but put down his cup gently, being acutely aware of having broken enough glass for one day. He said, "You want to know what I was going to say? I was going to say, 'Why don't you haul your fancy ass into the 'hood tomorrow and save some little old man from the neighbor's dog.' "

142

And then Marcie stood and *her* coffee cup *did* go over, and she screamed, "You're a goddam lunatic! You're fifty-five years old and you're still as crazy as they come!"

"It seems to be the prevailing opinion," he muttered.

"You've been miserable for two years now, ever since we moved into this house. I made you *rich,* and you've never forgiven me. I want you *out,* and I want you out now."

"Fair enough."

"Pack a bag and go. Go back to your apartment and get whatever is going on out of your system. Daniel can stay with you a few nights a week. Is his bedroom still there or has *your* son, the one *without* a handicap, got one of his sluts stashed there?"

That was low, Donovan thought. It was so low that any response would be pointless. He said nothing except "Daniel's room is still there. So is Mary's."

"Then *go,* William," she said. "Just go. We'll talk tomorrow. We'll sit down with Daniel and tell him together that you and I are going to live apart for a while."

"Sure," Donovan said.

"You *will* keep looking for a cure for him?"

"Harder than ever, and he'll be with me every step of the way."

Marcie nodded, calmed down, and so quickly that Donovan wondered if separation wasn't what she wanted all along.

"Go," she said. "Just go."

And away he went.

An hour later William Donovan, Captain, New York Police Department, retired, returned to the apartment that had been in his family for four generations. It was quiet in there and sounded like he might be alone, though of course he knew he wasn't. At that time of day—ten in the morning—it was night-time for night bartenders.

He put his bag down on the couch and walked to the window.

There was traffic on the Hudson—a tugboat was pushing a fully loaded barge upriver, perhaps all the way to Albany. This was, as always, commercial traffic on the river, but there was new traffic as well. Half a dozen sailboats sailed happily along as if this big rumbling river was a vacation spot. A lone kayaker skimmed the eastern bank. The water was cleaner than ever, clean enough to kayak in it. But it was still the Hudson, and the apartment was still his, and the scent of relief was in the air.

"Who's there?" Rosie called from the other room.

"Who were you expecting?" Donovan said, heading toward his old bedroom.

"Lewis, is that you?"

"You're a generation off."

The lack of panic, the absence of fear, the silence, said that she knew who it was.

He shed his clothes as he went, and they were mostly off when he got into the bedroom. She lay there in the middle of the bed with the sheets pulled up under her chin. If she wore anything he couldn't tell. Nor did he care.

"Are *you* still here?" he asked, walking to his side of the bed.

"What's it look like?"

"Didn't I throw you out?"

"*She* threw *you* out, didn't she?" Rosie asked, a lilt to her voice.

"I left," he said. He grabbed the sheets and pulled them down. "Move over," he said.

She did as she was told.

He climbed into bed.

"Are you here to finish what we started a couple of hours ago?"

"I'm here to sleep."

"I forgive you for being a shit before."

"And I forgive *you* for amply demonstrating your famous sense of humor," Donovan said.

"I still hate you," she replied.

He made a grumbly noise. Then he said, "I still want you out of my apartment."

"Do I have to get out of your bed?"

"No. I'm going to sleep. Good night."

"You smell like beer," Rosie said. "Just like the old days."

"Hire a lawyer and sue me," he said. "I know one if you don't."

He turned away from her, arranged the pillow to his liking, and sunk his head into it.

She slid over and draped an arm over him.

"I'm going to *sleep*," he said.

"I'm going to gloat," she replied. And then she added, "You'll *thank* me for getting you off the glacier, baby."

"Good *night*," he said.

She rolled away from him and looked out the window. She smelled the smell of the river and said to the river, "I got my man back."

If the river replied, history holds no record.

Donovan was asleep.

The forty-eight hours that followed included enough meetings, discussions, angry moments, touching moments, and reassuring moments to make it seem that Oprah had become a contestant on *Survivor*. But in the end things calmed down, Donovan moved a vanload of stuff back into the apartment, and Danny helped. The situation with the boy was complicated—although he put up a brave front like he did concerning his paralysis, and appeared to be coping, his father knew there was pain and it would take a long time to make things right. But Donovan meant to make that happen, and a big, first step and one that seemed to thrill the boy was the prospect of partnering up with his father and Uncle Brian in solving crimes.

And so it came to pass that Donovan & Son were moving cautiously down the tunnel leading from the library to the Hub, moving toward the sound of human conflict. It grew increasingly louder, until at last Donovan recognized the sound of grunting, yelping, swearing, shattering wood, and the angry Brooklyn snarl of Brian Moskowitz.

"What's that, Dad?" Danny asked.

"I think that Uncle Brian is having a conversation with Mr. Keogh," Donovan said.

They walked along, and as they were about to enter the Hub, Donovan called out, "Hey, yo!"

Mosko looked from the quivering mound above which circled the buzzards, or so it seemed to the Captain, who moved quickly in a woefully unsuccessful attempt to block his son's view.

"Are they done talking?" Danny asked, angling nonetheless for a view.

"I *hope* so," Donovan said, loudly enough for it to sound like a plea.

Not quite ignoring his old boss, Mosko extended a hand to Keogh and, with a muttered "On your feet, fool," yanked him to what passed for a standing position.

The battered campus security man used a wrinkled shirt sleeve to wipe the blood from his lips. Around his feet was scattered—what was until recently—a crateful of records. The orange-cratey wood they were made from was toothpicks and tongue depressors.

"Who's winning, Uncle Brian?" Danny said, beaming at his own cleverness.

"Liverpool," Mosko snarled. Then he looked fondly at the boy and said, "Hiya, kid. I see your old man talked you into bringing him."

The boy's smile widened.

Mosko continued, gesturing at the pile of boxes and saying, "Me and your Dad want to talk to Mr. Keogh a bit more. We're just gonna go a bit down the tunnel there."

He nodded in the direction of the tunnel where Danny had previously found the bathroom, the tunnel to the journalism building.

Mosko said, "Look in this pile of paper and see what you can find. Anything. About fallout shelters. About Professor Franks. About bombs."

"About Mercury," Donovan said.

"Sure," Danny said, taking from its holder the three-foot device he used to pluck various things from the floor without leaving the Beast.

"Let's take a walk down here," Mosko said to the fat PI.

Keogh followed them across the Hub and into the tunnel in question. When they got far enough away to protect the boy from further gore, Mosko took Keogh's shoulders and slammed him against the tunnel wall.

"Time to talk," Mosko said.

"What about," Keogh replied.

"We gotta do this again. I mean, for the Captain's benefit. I mean, I can let him do it himself. He's my muscle now."

"What are *you?*" Keogh asked.

"The man who's gonna kick the shit out of you—"

"Again," Donovan said with a smile.

"And cuff you to the wall in my office," Mosko said.

"Whaddya want to hear?"

"What is Nurse Ratched—Marion Riggs, RN, PhD—doing working for Riverside University?" Donovan said.

"She takes care of Franks," Keogh said, once again using his shirtsleeve to wipe his mouth.

Donovan thought that the blood was gone, but then he thought not. Then he grabbed Keogh by the shirtfront with his left hand and cocked his right first.

"Okay, *okay,* she's there to keep him from shooting his mouth off," Keogh said. Then, cocking his head in the direction of Mosko, said, "I thought *he* was the muscle."

"We shape-shifted," Mosko said.

"The university doesn't want him talking nonsense."

"Like *what* nonsense?" Donovan asked.

"Like I don't know. He's an old man."

"They have pills for that," Mosko said.

"Aricept," Donovan said. "Alzheimer's. I have a bit of it myself. I get forgetful. Sometimes I forget that the NYPD frowns on torture."

He cocked his fist again.

"Hey," Keogh protested.

"Waterboarding is next," Donovan said.

"Whaddya want to know?"

"What happened that they don't want him talking about?" Mosko asked.

"Man, I don't *know!* They don't tell me. All I know is that it has something to do with the tunnels. His old lab . . ."

"Where the atomic bomb was invented, partly," Donovan said.

"And the tunnels. They don't want him messing around in the tunnels," Keogh continued. "God knows what they don't want him saying or finding."

"Like the old records I have Danny going through now," Mosko said.

"Like that," Keogh said.

"Why don't they just throw them out if there's something so damaging in there?" Mosko asked.

"It would to be too obvious," Donovan said. "You can't just

trash a hundred years of history. This ain't the days of the old Soviet Union."

To Keogh, Donovan said, "Didn't it strike you as odd that they would want a nice old man shut up so badly that they got you to put an armed guard on him?"

"What's odd?" Keogh asked. "This is New York."

"Everybody has a crazy old uncle," Mosko said. "I'm not saying that Franks is crazy, just—"

"That there are a thousand other ways to handle it," Donovan said. "They couldn't put him in a home or anything, but they could have, I don't know, let it be known that he was two meatballs short of a hero. Everyone would understand and no one would talk about it. The guy was a legend. So let him run his mouth about the A-bomb. They'd pat him on the back patronizingly."

"Instead, they got their security guy to hire Nurse Ratched," Mosko said.

"Look," Keogh said. "I get paid to do what they tell me. I don't get paid to think."

"This is a good thing," Donovan said.

Keogh snorted and wiped his lips on his sleeve again.

"Whaddya want from me?" he asked.

"I want you to tell me who hired you," Mosko said.

"Yeager," Keogh said.

"The provost of Riverside University," Donovan said.

"The guy in charge of the faculty," Mosko said.

"Franks is faculty," Keogh said.

Donovan turned his back on the man and said to the bricks, "What's this all about? What could he know that's so important?"

"Beats the hell out of me," Keogh said.

"Someone is *about* to beat the hell out of you," Mosko said. "What does this have to do with your homicide?"

"Beats the hell out of me too," Donovan said. "I just feel that it does."

"Me too," Mosko said.

Keogh said, "You know, guys, I got to ask why a man is found dead in the tunnels and Professor Franks is not supposed to talk about what went on in the tunnels, and in his labs, and whatever."

"*Now* you're thinking," Donovan said.

"I used to be a cop," Keogh replied.

Donovan and Mosko talked to the man for a while longer, having decided that either he wasn't so bad after all or was better at faking sincerity than they might have imagined. They had a *guy* conversation, which started out angrily and with a little bloodshed, turned to grudging understanding and offers to help one another, and wound up in the latest sports news.

Now buddies, the three men went back to the Hub to collect Danny. They found him sitting in front of the row of boxes, not far from the one that got crushed when Mosko threw his now-buddy on top of it. He held the steno pad that he routinely carried in a pouch that was affixed to one side of the Beast.

"What's up?" Donovan asked.

"Whatcha find?" Mosko asked.

Beaming, Danny said, "I found a missing year."

Donovan asked what he meant.

"There are boxes with records for years all the way back to 1965," he said. "But there's no 1988."

"Nineteen eighty-eight," Donovan said flatly.

"What are those records and how did they get out in the Hub?" Mosko asked Keogh.

"Security records," the man replied. "They were in the part of the tunnel near my Security office. They were up against the walls like all the other stuff around here."

"Why are they out here?" Mosko asked.

"You guys are looking for stuff, I thought there might be something in there," Keogh said. "These are logs and other records of university *security* issues, after all."

"And there's no record of 1988?" Mosko asked the boy.

"No, Uncle Brian."

"What happened in 1988?" Mosko asked.

"Nothing," Donovan said. "Nothing relevant, anyway."

"Willie Stargell got into the baseball Hall of Fame," Keogh said.

"Pappy Boyington died," Donovan said.

"I don't see either of those things having anything to do with this," Mosko said, indicating the Hub, the tunnels, and the collection of boxes.

"Why would 1988, of all years, be missing?" Donovan asked. "I can understand someone filching 1968 for its historic value, but 1988?"

"It's got to be important," Mosko said.

"I could Google it," Danny offered.

Donovan smiled at his son. "That's a good idea," he said. "When in doubt, Google it."

Danny twisted and looked around his chair at the several pouches he used to carry stuff in, and his face sank. "I left my notebook at home," he said.

"You gotta keep it with you, pal," Mosko said. "If you're gonna be part of the team, you got to bring your tools with you." He smiled and patted the boy on the shoulder.

"I'll do it tonight," Danny said.

"Fire up the computer and see what you can find," Donovan said. "Search on the keywords 'Riverside University' and '1988' and—"

"I *know* what to do, Dad," the boy said.

"I'll shut up now," Donovan said.

"About time," Mosko said.

The Captain turned to walk toward the wall, and as he did so he felt what he liked to call "a ripple in the Force." The air went still, it filled with gently throbbing knowledge, and his brow was misted with the beginnings of sweat as he turned to see the expression of wide-eyed amazement on the face of his beloved special son.

"Daniel?" Donovan said, and now the other men were watching too.

"Dad," the boy said, "that was the year that Professor McGowan disappeared."

Cautiously, Donovan said, quietly, "He disappeared twenty-one years ago."

The boy shook his head, then smiled, then laughed and said, "I was bored the other night and looked at your notes. You added it up wrong. It was twenty years ago."

"Your old man can't add two and two," Mosko said.

"I know," Danny said.

Donovan looked up at the ceiling, and said, "The year that Patrick McGowan disappeared."

19. THE ATCHISON, TOPEKA, AND THE SANTA FE

"You can't just barge in here," said a red-faced provost unaccustomed to being jumped by two cops.

"We just did," Donovan said.

"There are procedures. There are right ways and there are wrong ways."

"There are ways for you to tell us why you hired a bodyguard to keep Samuel Franks from saying anything," Mosko said.

"I didn't—"

"And what happened to 1988?" Donovan asked.

Yeager asked what he meant.

"There are security records for every year going way, way back, except for 1988," Mosko said.

"What has this got to do with—"

"The security department reports to you," Donovan said. "The people in charge of maintaining the building report to you."

"Just about everyone reports to you," Mosko said.

More red-faced than before, Yeager reached for his telephone and said, "You can't barge in here without my permission. I'm calling the university's attorney."

"Good idea," Donovan said.

"Nothing said in here would stand up in court."

"What, are you in charge of the law school too?" Mosko asked.

"Get out of my office!"

Donovan and Mosko were quiet for a moment, and then

153

Mosko said to Donovan, "Hear that?"

He cupped his hand in the direction of an inner door.

"Hear what?" Yeager asked.

"Someone cry out for help," Donovan said.

"*What?*"

"I heard someone call for help," Donovan said. "In Spanish."

"He yelled, 'Morocco,' " Mosko said.

"*Ayuda*," Donovan said.

"Whatever. Look, Provost, you got a big problem here. Within a very short period of time, a janitor was murdered and cried out for help before he died."

"And then I hear someone call out for help inside your office. And, by the way, behind another suspicious door," Donovan said.

It was dark wood and thick, with brass fittings. It looked like it belonged on a movie set or in the crypt of the chapel.

"On top of that, you hired an armed private investigator to put the muzzle on your Nobel Prize–winning physicist to keep him from talking about what—from talking about the tunnels," Donovan said.

"And *now* records from the year that Patrick McGowan disappeared are missing," Mosko said. "I got to say something, and I hope you appreciate the fact I'm gonna put it in academic terms—what the fuck are you people doing here?"

"The lawyer will want to hear this," said Yeager, his red face having turned white.

"Call him," Mosko said.

"Her."

"Oh *fuck*," Mosko said.

"What?" Yeager asked.

"This case has more connections than the Atchison, Topeka, and the Santa Fe," Mosko said.

"What's her name?" Donovan asked.

Confused, Yeager said, "Karen. Karen Bernstein."

Donovan sighed audibly.

"Your life nearly got a lot more serious," Mosko said. "Fortunately, you ducked that bullet."

"We all did," Donovan said.

"I'm calling Karen," Yeager said.

"I'm calling Eyewitness News," Donovan said. "They will want to hear all this."

"Eyewitness News loves the Captain," Mosko said.

"We talk all the time."

"And I'll bet they get here before the lawyer," Mosko said.

Yeager thought for a moment, rather a desperate one, Donovan was sure. Then he sat down behind his desk and said, "What do you want from me? What can you *possibly* want from me?"

"For starters, what's behind that door?" Donovan asked.

"Records. More records. Faculty records." Yeager sounded exhausted.

"Why didn't you tell me that weeks ago?" Donovan asked.

"Because I *forgot*," Yeager said.

"You forgot," Mosko said.

"This is a university. We keep the records of the world, of human civilization."

"And a few instances of the lack of it," Donovan said.

"It *does* happen," Yeager said. "Look in there. Go ahead and look in there. Take them down to the tunnels and bury them. I don't care anymore."

"What about McGowan? Was it 1988 he disappeared in?" Donovan asked.

"Was it 1988? It could have been 1988. Let me see. I've been in that apartment since . . . yes, it could have been that year. What else happened that year?"

"Pappy Boyington died," Mosko said.

"Willie Stargell got into the Hall of Fame," Donovan added.

"What else do you want to know?" Yeager asked, resting his head portentously on his desk.

"Franks," Mosko said.

The provost raised his head. Donovan thought it had grown the racetrack-shaped-impression of a paper clip.

Yeager said, "What am I supposed to have done now? Oh, muzzled him or something. Who is this bodyguard you're talking about? I thought he had a nurse."

"He has a nurse," Mosko said. "She has an automatic weapon."

Yeager put his head back down on the desk, but not before he used a manicured finger to flick away a paper clip. He said, "*Why* did I turn down Princeton?"

"Einstein was there," Donovan said. "Another connection to the atomic bomb."

Yeager yanked his head back up and said, "Look, we had a part in developing the atomic bomb. Are we proud of it? No. But it's in the history books and there's nothing I can do about it. We had a prominent scientist disappear without a trace. I can't deny that. It may not be in the history books now, but it *will* before you're done with this. Am I right?"

He was looking at Donovan, and then he looked away, perhaps at the reflection of the brass fittings on the inner door in the glass of an antique clock sitting atop his desk.

Donovan shrugged.

"*And* . . . we had a janitor murdered in one of the tunnels. That's a fact. I can't say it isn't, and I hope you catch the killer. Now, did I hire a bodyguard to keep Samuel Franks from talking? No, nothing keeps Samuel Franks from talking. I hired a nurse to keep him from falling down again . . . he has twice already—"

"And exsanguinating on the steps to the administration building," Donovan said.

"That's a word he picked up on *CSI*," Mosko said. "It means bleeding to death."

"I *know* what it means," Yeager said.

"Why does the nurse you hired to keep him from falling down carry an automatic weapon?" Donovan asked

"Maybe she lives in a rough neighborhood. Why don't you ask her?"

"We will," Mosko said.

Yeager stood, turned, walked to the inner door, and yanked it open. Even standing across the room, Donovan could see several library shelves filled with records, this time in vertical files. At least searching would be easier.

"Go inside and look if you want," Yeager said. "Take all day. Camp out in there. Just please do it after I've treated my migraine."

He pulled open a desk drawer. From it he pulled a plastic bottle. He shook two pills into his hand and swallowed them with a gulp of water from a bottle on the table. Then as he put the pills back in the drawer his countenance brightened and he picked up a credit-card-sized bit of plastic with a photo on it.

"Here, Patrick McGowan's faculty ID. The exterminator found it behind the sink as he was spraying for roaches. I was going to give it to you but forgot when you barged in here."

"I didn't have a photo of him," Donovan said, handling the thing as if it were a great treasure.

"Now you do, and now I have a migraine. Will you go?" Yeager asked.

McGowan looked Irish, with reddish brown hair, a large forehead, and a devilish smile.

"I don't know how to thank you," Donovan said, as if the man wasn't a suspect in multiple crimes.

"Boric acid," Mosko said.

"What?" Yeager asked.

"Kills cockroaches," Donovan said. "I'll buy you a truckload."

Donovan had a container of coffee and he stared into it and tried to convince himself that he wasn't going mad from the complexity of the case on which his son and he were *just helping.*

"I'm not going mad," he said to himself.

As was so often the case in a bar, someone was listening, trolling for weakness.

"Yes you are," Jake said.

Donovan thanked him.

But Rosie said, "No, he's not. He's making sense at last. At long last, he's making sense."

"Doesn't look like it to me," Jake said.

"Why do you say that?" asked Marlowe, who was leaning over in front of Jake to get a bigger piece of the conversation.

"He's not drinking."

"The evening is young," Marlowe said.

Donovan sucked in his breath and let it out, saying, "I'm fascinated with the cult of drinking. This isn't an obsession or an addiction. It's a lifestyle. Ever see that bumper sticker that says, 'Work is the bane of the drinking class'?"

They all had.

"You guys sit in your dark rooms, your caves, watching the world go by, apart and aloof, sure of your own superiority. You voluntarily hover above the fray."

"We don't get skin cancer," Jake said.

"This is true," Donovan admitted.

Then he continued, "You stay apart, seeing everything, keeping the record of human civilization, of peace and war—"

"Twenty-nine missions!"

Jake saluted the No. 4 bus as it hummed down Broadway on its long march from the Cloisters to Penn Station.

"A while ago one of the mullahs across the street said that universities keep the record of the world. But he was full of shit, wasn't he? It's *you* guys who do. You watch the world go 'round, just like the Fool on the Hill," Donovan said. "Except you're the fools on the swill. And as for this place across the street . . ." Now that the bus had passed and Donovan had an unobstructed view, he gave Riverside University the finger. "Never has there been a more wretched hive of scum and villainy."

"Welcome home, honey," Rosie said, leaning to give him a peck on the cheek.

"I am *not* home," he snarled. "You have *not* got your man back. What you got is a reprieve until this case is over. Then you gotta get out of my apartment."

She looked around him at his friends and said, "This is how he *used* to be. Has he been like this *at all* over the past twenty years?"

"We only saw him now and then," Marlowe said. "He occasionally condescended to meet with us. But to answer your question, no, he was pretty much the distinguished gentleman of means with the trophy wife."

Donovan felt a burst of smoke coming out of his ears. "Trophy wife! I—"

"There's some question as to who was the trophy," Rosie said.

Marlowe added, "There *was* a head hung on the wall."

"You ready for a drink now?" George bellowed from down the bar, where he was listening to a story told by the guy who owned the local sports book. The stories told by Savas ("Duke") Dermirci were deadly, but so was Duke, in consequence of which people listened to them. It was said he blew away an unlucky schmuck who failed to keep his end of a bargain involving the Washington Redskins. No one knew if it really happened, but folks believed that it did, which is all that mattered

159

to the tobacco-stained old Turk.

"I'm working," Donovan yelled back.

"It sure looks like it," Marlowe said.

Duke raised a glass over his head and yelled at Donovan, "Hello, my friend."

Donovan waved his coffee cup at the man and bellowed a Canarsie-tinged, "How ya doon?"

"You're working?" Jake asked.

"I'm going back across the street in a while. I'm waiting to hear if Danny can come here after school, and if he does, we're visiting McGowan's old lab. You know, he used to work with frogs and now the lady who replaced him works with snails? The lab is on the downward spiral of phyla, which is about the same as my quest for McGowan."

"I thought that was on hold for a while," Marlowe said.

"It is and it ain't. Officially, it ain't. But since his name keeps coming up in the same breath as the hunt for the person who killed Gregorio Paz—"

"It's on," Marlowe said.

"And until it's off or Danny can't make it uptown today or something, I'm not drinking," Donovan said.

"I wonder what happened to McGowan," Rosie said.

"He probably fell into a black hole from which nothing can escape," Donovan said. "Such as New Jersey."

Rosie smiled and Jake grunted.

Suddenly, Donovan had about him that kind of glow that oft encircles those who have just thought of something wondrous. He reached into a pocket, pulled out McGowan's old Riverside University ID card, and slapped it on the bar.

"Here," he said. "Patrick McGowan, the man, himself. Take a good look at it, 'cause I'm never gonna find this guy and the photo is going into my closet along with all the other stuff that didn't work out in my life."

He gave Rosie a wicked smile and patted her on the head. She stuck her tongue out at him.

Jake glanced at the picture, grumbled, "Another Irishman," and went back to staring out the window.

Donovan was about to accelerate the pat on the head to a squeeze of the shoulder, which he thought a change in attitude modest enough to show that he didn't hate her as much as he had been suggesting. But then came Marlowe's voice, which would hardly be startling in and of itself did it not have its own glow of discovery.

He said, "Oh, *him!*"

Donovan slowly, portentously, turned his head in the direction of the voice.

"Him?" he asked cautiously.

"He was just a kid at the time, but . . ." Marlowe cleared his throat. "He came to my end-of-the-world party!"

Donovan was struck dumb. It was one of the very, extremely few times. Further, his mouth fell open. Well, a little.

Marlowe held the card up in the air, swiveled toward the back of the room, and called out, "Hey Duke!"

"Whaddya want, Professor?" the man asked.

He seemed joyed to be called upon. Most people averted their eyes when he came into the room. No one voluntarily called his name. He came over, hitching his pants up, swaggering like an old gunfighter as the crowd of drinkers parted for him.

"Look whose face came to light," Marlowe said, handing over the card.

The Turk glanced at the face of Patrick McGowan. He scowled, then he growled, "That's the sonofabitch who stiffed me on the Redskins! It was the Superbowl. I remember. He bet big on the Broncos, and when Washington won he wouldn't pay up! What year was that?"

"It *has* to have been 1988," Donovan said flatly.

"Yeah, 1988, that was it! Hey Captain, did you find him?"

"Right now I want to find a change of underwear," Donovan mumbled.

" 'Cause when you do, let me know," Duke snapped, " 'cause I'm gonna kill him *again!*"

20. CHRISTMAS TREES WITH
RED BALLS ON TOP

There were many spots, dark as midnight at noon, where the elevated West Side Highway made shelter. Lairs for the lost. Donovan, Mosko, and Duke sat, ground-down copies of the *Daily News* shielding their butts from the machine oil, pigeon feathers, gravel, urine, and empty "40" bottles. Below and a distance away, a sewer outflow spilled water and whatever else into the Hudson.

"I hope you boys are comfortable now," Mosko said for the third time in an hour, his tough-ass Brooklyn attitude struggling to fully appreciate the moment.

"Ah, it's a simple old West Side soiree," Donovan said, handing his old partner a 40 of Ballantine Ale.

Said Duke, continuing a conversation that had been going on for some time, "I did not kill the man. I wanted to, but I did not do it. And why did I not kill him?"

"You're a gentleman," Donovan said, using a word that Duke favored.

The man nodded. "I'm a gentleman. You're a gentleman. And so are you, my new friend from Brooklyn, who also is a policeman."

"Oh, you *heard* that rumor," Mosko said.

"But this Irishman with the test tubes, this McGowan. He was not a gentleman. He bet on the Broncos in the 1988 Superbowl, and they lost by a large score."

"Forty-two to ten," Donovan said.

To Mosko, who had offered a quizzical look to the friend who had long admitted to being "sports impaired," Donovan said "I watch *football*. The Giants. Well, hope springs eternal, even in New Jersey."

He made a bad face at the land on the wrong side of the Hudson.

"How much did he bet?" Mosko asked.

"One thousand dollars."

"On a football game!" Mosko said. "He bet a grand on a football game!"

Duke shrugged. "He said he had some big thing—some discovery—that he was sure he would sell for a lot of money. But he needed . . . what did cowboys call it, a grubstake?"

"And he couldn't go to the university?" Mosko asked.

"It was hush-hush," the man said. "It was big, and he didn't want to share it with anyone."

"Universities skim half off the top of research grants," Donovan said.

"And he didn't tell you what it was?" Mosko asked.

"He said I wouldn't understand. You see, McGowan was not a gentleman. You would tell me, wouldn't you?"

Both detectives said that they would.

"He said only that it was a cure for something. I forget what. No, let me take that back. It had something to do with paralysis."

Donovan breathed in deeply, then exhaled loudly.

Duke said, "McGowan planned to sell his invention. He told me that I would get paid eventually. Twice as much. I would multiply my money many times over."

"And you believed him?" Donovan asked.

Duke took the 40 from Mosko. Then he said, "McGowan had a drug company that was interested, he said. I understand that this is not so unusual."

"In that case he was telling the truth," Donovan said. "When a big drug company can't discover something on its own, it often will buy someone else's creation and market it as its own."

"So I let him go," Duke said. "What am I to do? Kill him, and lose any chance of being repaid? And there's another reason to let him live. It's one thing when you kill the owner of a grocery store for welching on a debt."

Mosko gave him a sharp look.

"Not that I've ever done that. Maybe I've broken a leg or two. But kill someone, no, of course not. I threatened to, and I waved a gun at him—"

"Hand it over," Donovan said.

As the man reached for the automatic weapon tucked in his belt in the back, Mosko drew his own.

But Donovan held his arm. "It's fake," he said.

"I make my own decisions these days."

Duke handed over a mean-looking automatic pistol. Donovan scanned it, popped the magazine in and out, then said, "A fake. A movie prop. Where'd you get it?"

"There was a film shooting in Washington Heights," Duke said.

Mosko put his weapon back in its holster.

"That thing is gonna get your head blown off one day," Donovan said.

"It will keep me from being arrested for possession of an unlicensed firearm. They can't put you in jail for possession of an unlicensed fake gun. I use it to frighten people. That is all. You know this, my friend."

Donovan nodded, then asked, "Did you threaten to kill McGowan?"

The old Turk smiled and said, "Of course I did, and where people could see it, too. The word spread and they are afraid of me to this day. But I did not kill the man."

Donovan nodded and looked out to the river. A mass of green

goo was spreading from the Jersey side.

Duke continued, matter of factly saying, "I told him to get lost. To pretend to be dead."

"I need more underwear," Donovan said.

Mosko smiled. Then he said, "He did it, right?"

"Sure. He pretended to run away. He knew that I could find him. That is to say, I *thought* that I could find him. So if you *do* locate the man turn him over to me. I will kill him for real this time."

"Anything else you want?" Mosko asked.

"No, I am *good,* as it has become fashionable to say. There is one thing more that occurs to me, however."

"Let's hear it," Mosko said.

"McGowan was eager to disappear. He told me that he was afraid he was going to be killed anyway."

"What?" Donovan asked.

"What he said was this, and perhaps it is important to you. He said, 'They want me dead. You see, I found out about it.' "

"Found out about what?"

Duke tossed his hands up. "I am not a mind reader. This is what the man told me."

"You have *no* idea?" Mosko asked.

"Not a one. Who would have wanted him dead other than me?"

"Found out about *what?*" Donovan asked, addressing his question to a white-flecked pigeon feather that a bit of wind had lifted up from the gravel and moved half a foot down the hill.

"What could a college professor who studies fucking *frogs* know that could get him killed?" Mosko asked.

"It wasn't football," Duke said.

"Somebody, presumably at the university, wanted him dead," Donovan said. "He needed money to get away and start a new life. So he made a losing bet . . . hardly the first time someone did that. He lost the bet. Unlucky. Then you offered him the chance to get away, which bolstered your reputation as a tough-ass head breaker."

Duke smiled, but as he did he looked nervously out of their hiding place to see if anyone was watching. "Anyone sees me with you gentlemen and that's the end of my reputation," he said.

Mosko picked up a pigeon feather and offered it to the late-afternoon breeze. As it fluttered off, he said, "I'll bet that whoever wanted to kill McGowan did so in 1988."

Donovan looked at him and nodded. "In 1962 McGowan goes to Marlowe's end-of-the-world party. A quarter century later, someone wants him dead. What the hell happened at Riverside University in 1988? I must get my research arm to look into this," he said.

"I can't find anything, Dad," said the research arm, tapping a finger of the left hand on his notebook while steering the Beast with his right. "I Googled everything you and I could think of, and I showed you the results. You said it was nothing. Maybe Uncle Brian is having more luck," Danny said.

Mosko and a team of detectives were going through the records that came from the room just off Yeager's office. They had them spread out on a conference table not far down the hall from the provost's office.

At the same time, Susan T. Raymond, PhD, awaited Donovan & Son in her lab—once McGowan's lab.

Donovan took it as a sign of his incipient madness that he distrusted women who used their middle initials.

When father and son walked in, they found a bright and sparkling new laboratory, clearly upgraded regularly, that was eons above others he had seen. There was far more electronics than glass, and anything that came close to resembling a test tube had been put far away, he supposed. Donovan was reminded of a high-end electronics store that hummed vaguely and was attended by figures in white coats.

One of whom was the striking Dr. Raymond, an athletic brunette who was far too good-looking to be a scientist in anything but a television show, no matter her six decades on the planet. She moved lithely, like a dancer or a model, flowing across the floor even when extending her hand to greet a retired policeman and his son.

"Hi, I'm Susan Raymond," she said, shaking in turn Donovan's hand and his son's.

If she thought it odd that the famous detective's sidekick was a boy in a wheelchair, she did an exquisite job of hiding it.

"Bill Donovan," he said, "And this is my son, Daniel."

"Hi," the boy said, smiling and pointedly drumming the fingers of his left hand on the cover of his notebook. That was one way he warned people not to underestimate him, Donovan knew.

"I hear that you are trying to find out about Patrick," she said.

"Patrick, yes, about Patrick," Donovan said. "So you knew him."

She nodded. "We did some work together early on . . . stem cells for nerve regeneration, but we had our individual interests and went in different directions. I was more interested in the science end, do you know what I mean?"

"No immediate practical application," Donovan said.

She smiled. "That's right. We like to say that if there's a clinical application, we're not interested. We pursue matters of scientific interest simply because these things are good to know."

"And 'Patrick'?" Donovan said the name in such a way as to accent her familiarity with the man.

"He was a bit more inclined to look for practical uses for his research," she replied.

"And were there any?" Donovan asked.

"Some, but not as many as he thought, in retrospect. He was pretty sure he had a molecule that could initiate cell differentiation of the type he wanted in vivo . . . in frogs . . . but I'm not so sure."

Donovan asked why she said that.

She replied, "If it was that easy, it would be a whole industry by now. He had some interesting leads, and who knows where he would be by now had he not disappeared. That, I understand, is what you are interested in—where he went."

"That's it."

"We're trying to find him," Danny added.

She said, "I don't know how much I can help you. We didn't have a personal relationship unless you count having coffee together in the lab. I really knew nothing about him, other than that he was a meticulous researcher with some good ideas."

Looking around, Donovan said, "This was his lab?"

She nodded. "His was twenty years ago, so you understand that it was nowhere as advanced. I had it gutted and rebuilt from the bottom up. I'm afraid that there's nothing remaining of the original."

"Nothing at all?" Donovan asked.

"What about the kitchen?" Danny asked.

They looked at him.

"Where you had coffee," he added.

"The *kitchen*," she said, clearly amused by her failure to come up with that possibility. "Yes, you're right . . . we couldn't have coffee in here, in the actual lab, not to mention the hideous sopaipillas he bought up on Broadway."

"Where's the kitchen?" Donovan asked.

Father and son followed her down a short hall, which, unlike

169

the lab, was plastered with bulletin boards and randomly Scotch-taped-up announcements and takeout menus. Announcements of visiting lecturers from Oxford and Berkeley mingled with Dilbert cartoons and photos from someone's trip to Easter Island.

The kitchen, such as it was, was at the end of the hall adjacent to an exit to a stairwell. It was a small room, just big enough for an archaic fridge, a onetime typewriter desk atop which sat a microwave, a small sink, and a four-person table. The latter was old-fashioned Formica with aluminum trim that was separating from the top in several places.

On the wall above the table was yet another bulletin board, this one old corkboard that was set inside a wood frame. On this board was anything but bulletins. Mostly there were business cards, concert tickets for sale, a "take it if you could possibly want it" teenybopper CD, and a handful of *Doonesburys*. Nearby was an old, white plastic wall-mounted phone. An ancient coffeemaker stood proudly on its own platform, an old, small bookshelf now holding coffee packets, filters, sugar, and Cremora.

Smiling, she said, "The equipment in *here* is original. Would you like some coffee?"

Donovan didn't, but Danny stared at the fridge intensely enough to earn himself a can of Diet Coke.

"You sat at this table when you had coffee?" Donovan asked.

"Yes, the very same. Is it important?"

"Where did McGowan sit?"

Donovan asked that while bending over, scrutinizing the layer of scrawls and scribbles along the wooden bulletin board frame.

Catching on, she indicated the side where the Captain stood. She was watching him inspecting the frame, and added, "Yes, that's him. He doodled Christmas trees. Little ones with red balls on top. He doodled them everywhere."

"I know," Donovan said.

"He made me crazy," she added.

"Did Mr. McGowan do that, Dad?" Danny asked.

"I think so."

"I've seen them," he said.

"I know . . . on those papers I was looking at in the basement of the library," Donovan said.

"Someplace else too," the boy continued.

"We have Christmas trees in the house," Donovan said. Then, fumbling, added, "In the apartment, wherever we happen to be."

"Someplace else too," Danny insisted.

Donovan was preoccupied with the frame, and sat down where McGowan sat daily two decades earlier. He ran a finger along the frame, atop the doodles, and there were many in several hands. But Donovan knew McGowan's handwriting, or hand*scrawling*, and focused on those made by him. In addition to the Christmas trees that seemed to be in a jumble everywhere, there were several alphanumeric sequences. One predominated. It was made using a firmer hand, and Donovan wrote it down. It was: GT74BY88GQ-a

He read it off to his hostess, who shrugged. "I have no idea what that is," she said.

"He never said anything?"

"We had *coffee* here," Dr. Raymond said. "I didn't know everything about Patrick. I told you what I know."

"There were no warning signs that he might disappear? Like, coming early in 1988?"

She sighed in a kind of exasperated way, and said, "Really, I—no, I don't know anything that can help you."

Donovan persisted. "That's all you know? That's all you saw him do? You worked or you had coffee and that was it."

"Captain—"

"Where did he have *lunch?* With you?"

"No, he liked to be alone a lot. He brought a sandwich and ate it in—"

She stopped then, apparently aware that she did, in fact, possess more information than she thought.

"You were about to say . . . ?"

"In the tunnel. He liked to have lunch alone in the tunnel."

Father and son looked at one another and then, without being asked, she said, "This way."

She led them out of the kitchen and through the stairwell door. She showed them around to the dark space behind the stairs, where the wall held an old iron door quite identical to the one behind which Donovan and son found the body of Gregorio Paz.

Danny said, "Should I call Uncle Brian?"

"I don't think it's necessary this time," Donovan said.

He stepped up to the door and grasped the handle.

"It's open," Dr. Raymond said. "One of my postdocs kicks a soccer ball down there sometimes."

"Yeah?" Danny exclaimed.

"Maybe he'll want a match," Donovan said, and yanked the door open. There was nothing there, just tunnel, no more. Like the others it was clean.

"I would *never* go down there," she said. "Not after that man was murdered. Is that why you're interested? Are you investigating the murder?"

"No, that's Uncle Brian's job."

He explained who that was.

"Danny and I are here looking for McGowan," Donovan said.

"Mostly," Danny added.

21. THEY SET ON YOU LIKE
THE FOX ON THE HOUNDS

"The records seem to be complete," Mosko said.

"For 1988?" Donovan asked.

"The same."

"What do they show?"

"Nothing that you and I can use," Mosko said. "The guy kept to his normal schedule, taught one class himself and supervised two RAs who taught two more classes . . . What's an RA?"

"Research assistant," Donovan said. "They're the doctoral candidates who actually do the teaching when the big-name professor can't tear himself away from his laboratory or the bar at the Faculty Club."

"Thanks. He also supervised two postdoctoral fellows. I can figure out what that one is."

"You're a good man. I taught you well."

"In summary, there's nothing in the records in that room behind Yeager's office that helps us at all."

Donovan asked if there was any indication that the files had been tampered with, and Mosko answered in the negative. "That's all we got, man . . . McGowan still disappeared and we don't know why. That is, unless you can figure out some connection between what you learned in the lab and what we know already, which ain't much."

"Dunno," Donovan answered. It was getting toward the end of the day, and he was tired. He had sent Danny home to the

173

townhouse and was trying to stay awake long enough to take care of some family matters.

"What about that number he doodled in the kitchen of that lab?"

"I asked Danny to check it out for me. You'd be surprised what kind of stuff pops up if you do a proper online search. He's good at computer stuff," Donovan said.

"The best. You gotta be proud of him," Mosko said.

"I'm proud of the whole fuckin' lot of you," Donovan replied.

"What's that number again?"

Donovan took one of his business cards out of his pocket. He had written the number on the back. He read it off: GT74BY88GQ-a.

"It's not a vehicle identification number," Mosko said.

"Too short. Besides, McGowan didn't own a car," Donovan said.

"And who do you think he was talking about when he told Duke that someone was out to kill him because he knows about *it?* What the hell is *it?*"

"What the hell are the Christmas trees?" Donovan asked.

"Say what?"

"The guy doodled Christmas trees. He doodled them everywhere. Little trees with red balls on the tops."

"So what? I doodle little red Corvettes," Mosko said. "What do you doodle?"

"I don't," Donovan said.

"Bullshit."

"I don't."

"Come on, out with it," Mosko said.

Donovan paused for a moment, then said, "Wheelchairs. I doodle wheelchairs."

Mosko's face dropped into a sort of fleeting sadness, then he clapped Donovan on the shoulder and said, "You'll get there."

"I hope so."

"Hey, speaking of your spawn, I—"

"My *what?*"

"Your kids. I commandeered the other one."

"Lewis? Lewis is working for you now?" Donovan asked.

"Just until Paz is over. I need someone with street smarts who knows this stretch of Broadway," Mosko said.

"He knows every *waitress*," Donovan said.

"I heard that."

"He's got a regular one now. I forget her name. Wait—Tina! No, hold on. It's something else. She works in the Cuban joint up on a Hundred and Forty-seventh."

"Waitress?"

Donovan shook his head. "She's the maitre d'. The hostess. He's spending most nights at her place. I think he was embarrassed suddenly being back with his parents."

"Like he moved back in," Mosko said.

Donovan nodded. "Except *he* moved *us* back in."

Mosko sighed audibly, and said, "I gotta talk to you about that, bro'."

"Yep," Donovan said, nodding profusely. "I gotta talk to me about that too."

"C'mon, I'll drive you home."

They walked down Broadway a few blocks past the campus, to the spot where Mosko had left his red 'Vette by a broken fire hydrant, an NYPD windshield sticker left to protect it from tickets given by zealous young police persons such as Lewis Rodriguez.

As Donovan slid into the passenger's side, Mosko made his usual circumnavigation of the vehicle, ever on the prowl for wet leaves and other tree detritus as well as such outrages as pigeon shit. Finding nothing more serious than a sodden ATM receipt,

Mosko got behind the wheel and roared up the engine.

"This thing still running good?" Donovan asked.

"Yeah, it survived the fact that you drove it once," Mosko snarled.

"I drove it two blocks, and that was four or five *years* ago."

"My baby has a long memory. So look . . ." He paused just long enough to get the car out of the parking spot and headed south on Broadway. "Remember we were talking about Rosie's moving back into your life?"

Donovan remembered.

"What are you doing about that?" Mosko asked.

"Nothing."

"Nothing?"

"What's to do?"

"The woman is in your *bed*, man," Mosko said.

"And the tragedy is . . . ?"

"You got a multiracial babe in the Village and now you got a Cuban babe in Harlem. Are you *ready* for this?"

"Ready for what, sleep? That's what I'm doing. For one thing, she sleeps in the afternoon when I work and I sleep at night, when she works. More or less."

"I know a gentleman wouldn't ask, but . . ."

"None has," Donovan replied with a grin. "The answer is no, I'm not having sex with her, nor am I going to, at least not until the dust settles on my marriage."

Mosko turned right at the McDonald's on the corner of 125th and Broadway and headed west toward the river. He drove past the Cotton Club, then he made a left and went up the ramp onto Riverside Drive.

"It's not a question of sex, it's a question of what's right," Mosko said. "You were jumped and that's it."

"Jumped?" Donovan asked.

"Yeah, jumped. They set on you like the fox on the hounds,

or is it the other way around?"

"I'm not sure."

"I mean, you love your son, but Christ, man, he moved his mom back into your apartment without even telling you. She moved herself into your bar. What's next, do you know?"

Donovan watched a jogger tying her shoes on one of the decorative benches flanking Grant's Tomb.

"I'm sure you'll tell me," he said.

"Your wallet, man. The next move is into your wallet."

"Look, it's my son and his mother, explain how that's wrong," Donovan said.

"Yeah, but—"

"There's nothing going on here that can't be explained on the grounds of family, or the times we live in. First, Rosie *is* someone I should have married, and might have if it wasn't too much trouble for her to mention being pregnant."

"There *is* a little bit of an attitude on her, isn't there?" Mosko said with a smile.

"You might say that. Now, she claims that she came back into my life after noticing that I was mortal. The fact that it was Lewis who saved my life the last time someone tried to blow my head off kind of adds weight to that argument."

"I guess."

"But y'know, I have this big apartment that I wasn't living in at the time, Lewis *was* living in it but spending most nights with Nina—"

"Tina, I think you said," Mosko replied.

"Whatever her name is," Donovan said. "So the apartment is available and Rosie needs a place to stay until she can move back into her old one, and I'm still living in the Village, and who gives a rat's ass if Rosie slides back into my old bed for a few weeks."

"She told you she lost the apartment in Union City," Mosko

said. "Did you believe her?"

"Yes. But I still checked out her story. Remember Bob Spado?"

"The sheriff guy over there?"

"I called him. Her story checks. A developer bought her building and tossed everyone out. It makes sense that she would move back to the city. She has a son here—"

"And an ex old man who also has a lot of money," Mosko said.

"That's not important," Donovan said.

"It's not to *you*, my friend, but to the rest of the world a couple of extra bucks don't hurt."

"And they can fucking *have it*. I'm so tired of this money thing. There's a reason that I don't like rich people, and it's simple—they rarely do anything good with it. There is an occasional exception. Right now, Bill Gates can do no wrong in my book. *Let* Microsoft plunder and pillage its way through the personal computing market. I don't give a rat's ass. The other one, too. Warren Buffett. Damn, if those two dudes go broke giving away their money for the common good, I'll pay for their fucking funerals. Marcie and Daniel are taken care of. I was taken care of before this whole thing began, because captains with thirty-plus-year careers retire with good bucks and I had— have—a rent-controlled apartment. Now that my rich lawyer wife laid a stock portfolio on me as a Father's Day present, tell me why my other son and his mom shouldn't be taken care of, too."

A dozen or more kids were raising a ruckus on the playground equipment at Riverside and 104th Street. Donovan watched them as Mosko drove by.

"I'm taking care of the people who matter to me," he muttered. "Other than that, I'm hiding it under a rock. If *you* need anything, you let me know."

"Got gas money?" Mosko asked, holding out a palm.

Donovan told him yet again to go fuck himself.

"Rosie gave me a son," Donovan said, a bit wistfully. He also sighed, perhaps a bit too loudly.

"That's nice," Mosko said.

"And she still has a goddam fine ass," Donovan said.

Laughing, Mosko said, "I thought you said you weren't having sex with her."

"I never said forever," Donovan replied as the Soldiers and Sailors Monument, across from which he lived, hove into view.

The fire in the fireplace didn't roar, exactly. It was somewhere between a roar and a sputter. But it wasn't chill enough an evening to warrant a blazing fire, and anyway it was the idea that counted. Donovan sat back on the couch with his feet up, listening to his eldest son apologize.

"I'm really sorry," he said. "I didn't think you would be upset."

"I'm not upset exactly," Donovan replied. "I just would have liked to have known ahead of time."

"Should I have told you that Mom needed a place to stay?" Lewis asked.

"In a word, yes."

"Sorry," he said again.

Donovan stretched and looked at the ceiling long enough to see cobwebs. Lewis's housekeeping demands clearly were of a level lower than Marcie's. Thankfully.

"You don't think I would have said 'no,' do you?" Donovan asked.

"No."

"Because I wouldn't. I just don't take surprises as well as I once did. Yes, I would like to have known. And yes, I'm glad you did it. I missed her. Don't tell her I said that."

Lewis smiled, looking relieved. Then he said, "I hear you had a good time the other morning."

Donovan returned the smile, and added, "Is that how she depicted it? A good time. Well, then she really hasn't changed at all. And I'm glad for that."

"She says you haven't changed either."

Donovan patted his hairline, saying, "She's kind. Look, there's something I want to get straight with you."

"Okay," Lewis said, abruptly sitting up a bit.

"Actually there are two things. The first is that there ain't no promises as to what happens with your mom and me. Everything seems pretty cool now, but we have to see. We've been 'back together,' if you want to call it that, for all of forty-eight hours, and we're on really different schedules."

"She'd like it if you hung around the bar more," Lewis added.

Laughing, Donovan said, "Do you have *any idea* how long ago I first heard someone ask me to quit the force and go work in a bar? It was your mom—in 1981 or 1982, if memory serves. Your mom asking me to go work at Riley's was where this all started, everything! Well, I didn't do it then and I'm not doing it now. As much as I talk it up with my old friends, I really don't like drinking that much. And hardcore drinkers are a smug bunch of assholes who are as sure of their own righteousness as any pope or rabbi. Rosie will see enough of me."

"Okay."

"What I want you to understand is that your mom and I will work out our relationship together. The way things stand now, I think it best that she stick with her plans and move back into her old apartment."

If Lewis was disappointed, he hid it well.

Donovan continued, "She knows I feel this way. We've talked about it. And we'll talk about it plenty more."

"Okay."

"So . . . that's one thing I wanted to say."

"And the other?" the young man asked cautiously.

"My friend—your friend and now, I hear, partner—Lieutenant Wonderful, thinks that money may become an issue now that I'm on my own and your mom is sort of back in my life."

"What sort of issue?" Lewis asked, also cautiously.

"You may need more," Donovan said. "Your mom, too."

"Why would I need more?"

"Well, you seem to be moving in with . . . with . . ."

"Rita," Lewis said.

"Are you moving in together?" Donovan asked.

"Kind of."

"And you'll be paying rent."

"We both will," Lewis said. "And I make a good living."

"I know how much you make," Donovan said, pointedly.

"Dad—"

"Brian thinks that you may want money, and I think that you'll be too shy to ask for it, so let's get this out of the way now." Donovan pulled something out of his shirt pocket, and as he did so, said, "I'd like to get money off the table. It's burning a hole in my karma and I don't want it to keep coming up in conversation. We'll take care of details at some point, but let me say right now that you have nothing to worry about. Like, for the rest of your life have nothing to worry about. You won't be hugely rich . . . I'm not either. You'll be comfortable. The catch being . . ."

His father was smiling, so Lewis appeared worried no longer.

"Don't go around showing the world that you have bread. And try to do some good in the world. At least, as the doctors supposedly, say, do no harm. Continue to be a good person. You are already, so I'm not worried. I have this motto that good people should live forever and that justice should be applied when bad people prevent that from happening."

"I'll do that."

"I'd also like you to help me with my projects, which at the moment and maybe forever will be helping find a cure for your brother."

"I promise," Lewis said.

Donovan smiled and said, "Take this. Put it in your wallet."

Lewis took the card and looked at it. "I've never seen an American Express card that looked like this."

"It's a special kind. I have an arrangement with them. You can buy whatever you like, but if you start buying yachts I'll hear about it. Now stick it in your wallet. Take Rita to the Bahamas for her birthday."

"Okay!"

"*And buy food for the old lady down the hall* if that's what she needs," he added.

"You got it. And *thanks!*"

Donovan sighed and leaned back and stretched, looking again at the ceiling. "I like the cobwebs," he said.

"I'll get the broom," Lewis said, and made a motion to do so.

"Don't you dare," Donovan said. "Spiders have to eat too. And I hate mosquitoes."

Lewis laughed. Then he said, "I'm getting myself a beer. Do you want one?"

"No." Then he added, "I need you to do something."

"What?"

"Find out what stores along Broadway near the university sell sopaipillas and have done so for twenty years," he said.

"The sweet cakes?"

"Pastries, whatever they are," Donovan said.

"Sure. I guess it's important," Lewis said.

"It could be."

"I'll take care of it."

"I like having us all work together," Donovan said. "You, me,

Danny. My sons and me."

"Me too," Lewis said. "Are you sure you won't have that beer?"

Donovan said he was sure.

"Be right back."

The young man got up and, putting the card in his wallet as he walked, went through the dining room and into the kitchen. Donovan heard some clattering around . . . the fridge was old and would have to go, he thought, and then he thought better of it. It will do, he thought.

Then when he returned, along with a bottle of Blue Point Ale, Lewis carried his father's laptop. He handed it over, saying, "You have email on your Yahoo account."

Donovan took the laptop and peered at it. "It's your brother, staying up too late again."

Lewis took his cell phone from the coffee table and flipped through the menus.

Donovan opened his mail, read it, then laughed, then shook his head and leaned back and howled laughter at the cobwebs.

"What?" Lewis asked.

"Do you know what little Christmas trees with red balls on the top are when you put them together in an arrangement of threes?"

Lewis shook his head.

"A radiation hazard warning," Donovan said, laughing again.

"Dad?"

"And the number GT74BY88GQ-a? Any ideas? No, well, I couldn't figure out what it was either. But Danny could. He Googled it. I didn't know that product codes would show up on Google searches, but they do."

"What is it?" Lewis asked.

"A portable multi-channel detector," Donovan said. "A Geiger counter—a particular high-end brand that was introduced in the middle of the 1980s."

"This is about McGowan, isn't it?"

"Oh yeah," his father said.

22. A ONCE-PROMINENT
SCIENTIST WHOSE SOLE FLAW
WAS THAT HIS KNOWLEDGE OF
FOOTBALL SUCKED

Howard Bonaci's big white forensics van took up a prominent chunk of the campus. Forensics evidence gatherers prowled here and there, slipping in and out of buildings and in and out of tunnels carrying portable multi-channel detectors, while Provost Yeager stood, fuming, in the shadow of the Martin Luther King statue, which looked appalled, and Bill Donovan stood bent over admiring the trousers of a crime-scene investigator.

"This is wonderful, this is the invention that will save mankind," Donovan said to his young son.

"What, Dad?" the boy asked, using a vaguely exasperated tone of voice that was well beyond his years but familiar to anyone who ever worked with the Captain. At that moment, the exasperated included a hard-working forensics investigator who, when he showed up for work that day, clearly had no idea he would be Exhibit A in a discourse on the place of tools in twenty-first-century America.

Donovan pointed at the pants and said to Danny and anyone else who would listen, "There are loops to hold duct tape! Can you believe it, duct tape!"

"That's great," Danny said.

"Duct tape is one of the great inventions of the twentieth century," Donovan continued. "The world would have fallen apart ten times over were it not for duct tape. Duct tape can fix *anything*. Well, maybe not George W. Bush's place in history.

But the problem before was that the rolls were too big to hang on anything and too small to go around your wrist. So you were always leaving the roll on top of something and it would get lost or stolen."

"Are you coming to an end with this?" Mosko leaned over and stage-whispered. He had been standing tall and proud at the front of the van directing the traffic of detectives and technicians.

"Or it would fall on the ground and roll away," Donovan went on. "The rolls *roll* great. But now—in the twenty-first century, and thank God something good finally happened in it—they're making pants that have loops down the side for duct tape."

"They're for forensics tape, Captain," the man said.

"Doesn't matter. The loops could have been made for bagels. The point is they can hold duct tape."

He smiled at Danny, who looked away, a bit embarrassed.

"Can I go to work now, Chief?" the technician asked Mosko.

"Sure," Mosko replied, and turned, a bit sheepishly, to find his old boss grinning at him.

"Chief?" Donovan said. "*Chief!* I like the sound of that. Chief Moskowitz."

"You're very pleased with yourself today, aren't you," Mosko said.

"I'm pleased with my *son*," Donovan explained. He rested his hand on Danny's shoulder. The boy no longer appeared to be embarrassed.

It was a bright sunny day and the Frisbee players were out, skimming their plastic disks a handful of yards above the tunnel system that now was feared to be a hive of radioactivity left over from the days of atomic bomb research. On the steps to the administration building, students with laptops worked alongside students with iPods and everyone flirted. So far, word hadn't gotten out just what the NYPD was looking for down below, but the fear of that happening was great enough to bring out Yeager and a retinue of university officials.

"This is going too far," he said, his voice little better than a stammer.

"Actually, it ain't gone far enough," Mosko replied, secure enough in his command to taunt Yeager with the deliberate use of bad grammar. "We been much too easy on you guys. The ways I sees it there's been nucular radiation—"

"Hold your voice down, *please!*" Yeager pleaded.

"There's been *nuclear radiation* down there since before the Captain here was born, and that's going back aways."

"Thank you," Donovan said.

"What I think is that you hid all this atomic shit down there in the tunnels, put thousands of lives—tens of thousands of student lives at risk—and you covered it up. You thought that if you kept Sam Franks from shooting his mouth off that no one would know, and you sat on him for years. But what happened? A guy named Patrick McGowan—who was afraid of what the atomic age was doing to us all and went to an end-of-the-world-party when he was a kid to show it—this guy stumbled over the fact that his lab was right next to ground zero of nuclear testing in the Isle of Manhattan."

"What happened, were his stem cells dying inexplicably?" Donovan asked.

"That was twenty years ago!" Yeager protested.

"What's the half life of uranium?" Donovan asked out loud.

"Four point five billion years," Danny answered.

His father thanked him.

Mosko continued, "So McGowan goes out and buys some high-end Geiger counter and starts poking around. What did he find? Well, whatever he found scared him enough to tell people what he 'knew about it' and worry that someone was going to

187

kill him. And then he disappeared, without a trace, remember, leaving only an ID card and an apartment—"

"Both of which were in your possession as of the other day," Donovan added.

"This is *crazy!*" Yeager cried.

"What did you do, doc, kill him and bury him down below?" Mosko asked. "My colleague here"—he rested a hand on Danny's shoulder—"found where the old john had been bricked up. What happens if we tear out those bricks? Do we find the body of a once-prominent scientist whose sole flaw was that his knowledge of football sucked?"

"Oh my God," Yeager said, reaching behind him as if looking for a chair, then scrambling to where he could sit on the steps leading up to the administration building.

"I hope we find something," Mosko said quietly.

"No shit," Donovan replied.

But they didn't find anything, and half a day later were standing there, empty-handed, not quite eating crow but maintaining a much lower profile with their righteous outrage.

That was hardly the same for university officials, who by then had grown more lawyers and taken the lead in terms of outrage.

"You found *nothing!*" Yeager said, nearly yelling, his fear of being overheard not even a distant memory.

"We found traces of radiation," Mosko said.

"Traces. That's exactly right. You found *traces*, which occur everywhere. Background radiation is everywhere, in the soil, in foods—"

"In the tunnel leading up to Franks' lab," Donovan said. "Particularly there."

"Well, it *was* a place where nuclear research was conducted— half a century ago. But I saw the numbers your people picked up down there on their Geiger counters, and they'll all within code. There's no more radiation down there than you'd find in a dentist's office with the X-ray machine."

Mosko shuffled his feet.

Karen Bernstein, the attorney retained by the university to handle criminal issues—normally on the level of students getting drunk and being arrested for urinating in public—joined Yeager then. She wound up and said to Donovan, "The assumptions you made in getting your warrant are unsupported. What you have is hearsay regarding a circumstance—high radiation levels—not a crime. And this is a circumstance thought to have occurred twenty years ago and alleged by you on the basis of hearsay from a man who disappeared twenty years ago. You made a mistake, Captain."

"*He's* the boss," Donovan said, indicating Mosko.

Only the presence of witnesses prevented the occurrence of something really ugly.

Instead, Mosko turned to the lawyer and said, "He's right, I *am* the boss and I say that our warrant gives us twenty-four hours, of which we've used six. If you want to stick around and watch, that's fine. Just stay outside the yellow crime-scene tape. I'll assign an officer to assist you."

That didn't turn out to be necessary, and when the retinue from the university administration had repaired to the Faculty Club for drinks, Mosko told Bonaci to redeploy the troops as best as he saw fit but to go over the entire tunnel system once more, lest they missed something.

"I think we ought to go back to the kitchen in McGowan's old lab," Donovan said.

"Why?" Mosko asked. "We did it once already. It's the same as everywhere else. Low-level background radiation, same as you'd find in a dentist's office."

"Danny thinks we ought to check the tunnel that we found yesterday, the one leading away from McGowan's old lab."

189

"We checked it," Mosko said.

"Who checked it?" Donovan asked.

"One of the techs. Is it important?"

"Did one of *us* check it? I mean, the tech was looking for radiation, not whether the tunnel went to the Hub like everyone assumes, or is a gateway to an alternate universe."

Mosko grumbled, walked to the side of the forensics van, and gave it a powerful thump with his fist.

"Hey, yo!" he called out.

Bonaci stuck his head out the door and yelled, "Whaddya want?"

"Who checked the tunnel leading away from McGowan's lab?" Mosko asked.

"Mark."

"What'd he find?"

"Radiation," Bonaci replied. "Can I go now, you're interrupting me."

"How *much* radiation, Howard?"

"If I told you, would you know what I'm talking about?"

Donovan sighed. He said to Mosko, "This is where you get it from, isn't it? Paz died from weird shit in the brain. The radiation level is something we can't possibly comprehend."

To Bonaci, Mosko said, "Howard, you *do* have hard facts stuck somewhere in that avalanche of bullshit and attitude, don't you?"

"It stands up in court, doesn't it?" Bonaci said. "Are you done too, 'cause I'm still busy."

"Where did the fucking tunnel go?" Mosko asked.

"It went to the other building."

"Not to the Hub?"

"No, I just said it went to the other building."

"That being?" Donovan asked.

"The one next door. The physics place. It comes out right

next to the old guy's lab. You know, the one with a jumbotron in it."

Danny said, "Uncle Howard, a jumbotron is like the big TV in Times Square." He laughed.

"Then it's the Cyclone," Bonaci proclaimed.

"That's the roller coaster in Coney Island," Donovan said.

"Dammit, would you guys leave me alone. It's the big thing with the wire and tubes. It only has slightly higher radiation levels than the background levels everywhere else. Now if you don't mind—"

"Give Danny a Geiger counter, Howard," Mosko said.

Bonaci did so, emerging from his van with one of the gadgets and handing it to the boy. Then he said, "I'm glad to see that one of you guys knows what he's doing. Don't let your dad or Uncle Brian touch it, okay?"

"Okay," Danny said.

"They'll only break it. I'm going now."

And he got back inside the van and slammed the door.

"Can we go so I can use this?" the boy asked eagerly.

23. Mercury Rising

McGowan's old lab was closed. It was closed except for Susan Raymond, who sat in a chair blocking the way to the sensitive instruments and snail containers.

"Not in here, not in here," she said.

"Not in there," Mosko said.

"We like snails and would do nothing to harm them," Donovan said as the three of them walked by and down the hall to the kitchen, followed by three detectives from Special Investigations.

When they got to the kitchen, Donovan and Mosko stayed out in the hall while the boy rolled around in the Beast, poking here, poking there, looking at the readout on the instrument. After a minute or two he stopped and turned to the grownups and said, "It's like Uncle Howard said."

"Okay," Mosko said, "the hall."

Again, Danny led the way up and down the hall. Again, the results were the same.

"It's background radiation," Donovan said.

"The tunnel," Mosko said.

Donovan went to the tunnel door and grabbed the handle.

Mosko said, "We checked the manufacturer's records. McGowan bought one of those gadgets in October of 1987 so he must have been using it from then on until he disappeared, which was late spring, right? Do you want me to help with that door, Gramps?"

Donovan made a hissing noise. Soon the tunnel door was open and Mosko stepped into it, followed by Danny, then his father, then the other detectives. As soon as he was in and got his bearings, Danny said, "This tunnel doesn't go in the direction of the Hub. The Hub is over there."

He pointed to the left.

"The Hub has nothing to do with all this," Mosko said. "We checked it up and down."

"This hall goes to the physics building," Danny said.

"How do you do that?" Mosko asked.

"Do what, Uncle Brian?"

"Find your way around in the dark. I can't tell one direction from another down here."

"Magnetite," Donovan said.

"Say what?" Mosko asked.

"Magnetite," Donovan replied. "Little bits of magnetic material found in the brains of dolphins and other critters that use the Earth's magnetic field to find their way around. All the Donovans have it."

"Oh, so that's how you know exactly where the donuts are," Mosko said.

"You got it."

Danny giggled.

Then as they walked along, he said, "The radiation is getting a little stronger as we walk. But it's still low."

"You'd expect it to increase as you get closer to Franks' lab, right?" Mosko asked.

"I suppose," Donovan said.

And that was how it turned out. As they moved out of sight of the tunnel entrance near McGowan's lab, they spotted the door leading to Franks' lab. And the Geiger readings continued to grow, but still were very low. Background radiation, maybe a trace more.

When they got to the tunnel exit, they pushed open that door to find themselves in the hall down which Donovan and Mosko first walked on their way to Franks' lab. And like that time, noise came from the historic facility. Some chatter. Some clanging and banging.

"The raccoons are in the attic again," Donovan said.

"Yeah!" Danny replied.

Mosko looked at Donovan and said, "Someone ought to publish a guidebook to you. 'Field Guide to Bill Donovan, a Handy Reference for Those Who Can't Figure Out What the Fuck He's Talking about at Any Given Moment.' "

Donovan ignored him.

To Danny, the Captain said, "Remember that time at Grandma's house when the raccoons were making all that noise in the attic, and you and I couldn't figure out what to do?"

"Yeah."

"Tell Uncle Brian what Grandma did to get rid of them."

"She got on a stepladder and cut a round hole in the bedroom ceiling. Then she put the vacuum cleaner hose on the exhaust end. Then she filled the hose up with moth balls. Then she stuck the hose in the hole she made in the ceiling and turned on the vacuum and blew the moth balls up into the attic."

"That got rid of them, didn't it?" Donovan said.

"They ran right out and never came back."

"Another operation successfully concluded," Donovan said.

Said Danny, "Uncle Brian, do you have moth balls?"

"My God, there are two of them!" Mosko said, pushing ahead and heading down the hall to Franks' lab.

Inside the lab, and looking none too happy about it, Marion Riggs, RN, watched as Samuel Franks worked on the tie rod that he had failed to reassemble correctly before. The detectives watched him from the door for a moment, until he dropped the thing again and it made another loud clatter on the floor.

"*Oy*," Franks said.

"Working on the problem of gravity again, Franks?" Donovan asked.

Franks turned and looked at the visitors. So did Riggs, who was none too happy about *them*, either.

"My friends!" he said happily. "Come in, come in. Did you find what you were looking for in the tunnels?"

Donovan and Mosko looked at one another. Then Mosko said, "We were hoping you could help us."

"And young Mr. Donovan, too," Franks said, shaking Danny's hand. "It is so good to see you, too."

"Hi," Danny replied.

"And you brought a Geiger counter. That's wonderful. What is it telling you?"

Danny looked down at the instrument, then up at the old man, and said, "Not much."

"Of course it's telling you not much. And that is because there *is* not much. There is very little radiation here, faintly above background. Trust me that we have been through this—conducted the experiment you are conducting today—many times over the years, many times."

Nurse Riggs said, "Dr. Franks, perhaps—"

"We are talking, please," he said politely.

Then to his guests, he said, "I heard that you would be searching the tunnels today, and so I came here to meet you. And I have something to say, something long overdue. I have a pot of coffee on. Would you like some?"

None of them would.

Franks sighed loudly and said, "A long time ago there was a madman on the loose in the world, seeking to destroy the world. We put an end to it, all of us. I played a small part, and I am proud of the part I played. But—"

Again Nurse Riggs butted in, saying "Professor! It is time to go home for your rest."

"We're *talking* here," Mosko said, not *quite* as politely as Franks did.

"It is time for him to go," she insisted.

Said Franks, with what appeared to be genuine sorrow, "Nurse, I was brought up in a different world, in Vienna a long time ago, and men and women behaved in certain ways that they do not anymore. I hear myself about to say something that I never imagined myself saying. You tell me that I must go, and I say to you, 'Go fuck yourself.' "

Silence fell from the ceiling.

Then Mosko beckoned one of his men forward, and said, "Jim, this woman is licensed to carry a nine millimeter, or says that she is. I would like you to check her license."

"You got it," the man replied.

Flustered, Nurse Riggs said "I—it must be in my car."

"You're not carrying your papers on your person?" Jim asked.

"I—unh, no."

Jim pulled back the side of his jacket, revealing his own weapon. He put his hand on it and said, "Ma'am, I would like you to show me your weapon, and then I would like you to take it out of its holster and I would like you to put it on the floor. Now, please."

Behind him, two other detectives put their hands on their weapons.

Danny was wide-eyed.

The nurse did as she was told, all the while muttering, "Oh God oh God oh God."

Then one of the detectives scooped up her 9mm and took her by the arm to lead her away.

Said Mosko, "Take her to her car and look at her license. Take her by the scenic route."

"The dark side of the moon seems about right," Donovan said.

"I just *knew* that you were a Pink Floyd fan," Mosko said as he watched the woman being led off.

"Thank you," Franks said, offering a polite little bow.

Mosko let out a big burst of air.

"That was *fun*," Danny said.

"Okay Franks," Donovan said. "*Veritas*. The truth shall set you free. You're not a doddering old fool but have been treated like one, and maybe you've been going along with it. Why? So you don't have to say what we're asking you to say right now."

"And here it is: What the hell has been going on at this school?" Mosko asked.

"It's been so long, and there is much confusion—what I did, what I feel, what I feel about ruining the reputation of this fine institution, what I feel about watching records be destroyed, what history feels—"

"What *happened?*" Donovan insisted.

"Ask your questions," Franks said.

"What was the big secret?" Mosko asked. "Was it about the radiation down here?"

"There *is* no radiation down here, none to speak of. That's the point. You have seen so yourself."

"How could there be no radiation down here?" Donovan asked. "This is where you did the isotope separation. It says so in the official history of this national landmark. I read, 'The Physics Laboratory of Samuel Franks on the Riverside University campus in New York is where scientists conducted the isotope separation that was an essential part of developing the nuclear weapon that ended World War II.' "

Franks giggled.

"That's what it *says!*" Donovan said.

The old man laughed. He said, "Here? Of course not, not *here!*"

"Why not?" Donovan asked, trying to imagine what was amusing Franks.

"Why, it was *too dangerous* to do the isotope separation on campus. There would be radiation. Think of all the students."

Donovan and Mosko looked at one another, and Danny looked at all three of the grown-ups.

"Where did you do it?" Danny asked.

"Why . . . we did it in Harlem."

The silence in that old lab rivaled that in the seconds before the first nuclear detonation in the New Mexico desert.

"You . . . did . . . it . . . in . . . Harlem," Mosko said, his wise-cracking Brooklyn persona having turned up ill and failed him.

"Where in Harlem?" Donovan asked.

Matter of factly, Franks said, "In the Mercury Building."

Once again, the two detectives speechlessly scanned one another's retinas.

"Mercury," Mosko then said, and quietly.

Donovan said, "I've looked at the map of all the buildings, both on campus and off. Riverside University has no Mercury Building."

More laughter, then Franks said, "We just *called* it that. In fact, it was an automobile dealership that had gone out of business because of the war. A dingy old place, dark as a tomb."

"Mercury automobiles," Donovan said.

"Suck," Mosko said, his Brooklyn persona having recovered and returned.

"Where was this dingy old place, dark as a tomb?" Donovan asked.

"*That* I really can't say," Franks replied.

"You have no idea?"

"I went looking for it several times. But it's one of those

198

things that have eluded me. I suppose this is because it wasn't a campus building and wasn't really important to us."

"A building in Harlem where you did the isotope separation wasn't important to you," Donovan said flatly.

"The *building* wasn't important," Franks said. "What was *done* there was important. I think it was on Amsterdam Avenue. No, it was Saint Nicholas Avenue. I'm just not sure. I was seldom there, and when I was they drove me."

"Mercury," Donovan said, a single word, and then he fell silent.

"This Mercury Building in Harlem would have been made dangerous by the radiation, wouldn't it?" Mosko asked.

"I suppose that some people could have been made sick," Franks said. "I doubt that it would have killed anyone."

"Not directly," Donovan said.

"You're not the first ones to ask me about this, you know," Franks said.

"That would have been McGowan," Mosko said.

"Yes. The same. A very pleasant fellow, I found him. He came around here with a Geiger counter, same as you. And I told him the same things that I just told you."

"He just wandered in?" Donovan asked.

"Yes, absolutely yes, exactly that. It was twenty years ago—"

"Nineteen eighty-eight," Danny said.

"He came to me. Asked something about the effect of radiation on stem cells."

"And you said?"

"That it would kill them," Franks replied. "It kills everything."

"And after you told him what you just told us, he did what?" Donovan asked.

"Oh, he was very excited. He went looking for the Mercury Building, but he couldn't find it either, and we thought maybe they tore it down, he did this, he did that—"

"He disappeared," Mosko said.

"Well, yes. He disappeared. And they were *very* angry with me for telling him the story."

"They told you to shut up and placed a guard on you to make sure that you did," Donovan said.

"We ended World War Two," Franks said. "We saved the world from a madman. It was worth making a few people sick in Harlem."

Franks seemed to be pondering the quiet around him. Then he added, "No one died."

"Gregorio Paz will be glad to hear that," Donovan replied.

Franks' face suddenly had the look of startled amazement, and he said, "I just remembered something. I also told that young man."

"Paz?" Mosko asked, just as startled.

"Why yes, him, the young fellow," Franks said. "He seemed so eager to know about the experiments, he was wide-eyed when I told him. So were you, Captain."

"Imagine that," Donovan said.

"He was *so* impressed that atomic bomb experiments actually were done here, *so* impressed. But he was such an honest and eager-looking young man that I felt I owed him the truth. I said, 'Why no, the really exciting work was done in the Mercury Building.' But of course I couldn't remember where it was then either."

"And next," Mosko asked. "What happened next?"

"He ran off just like McGowan did twenty years earlier. But this time I had been overheard talking."

"Your guardian," Donovan said.

Franks nodded and smiled. "I had dispatched her on yet another bogus mission, but she came back early and overheard me telling the story to the young man, Paz."

"That's when they started getting tough on you," Mosko said.

"Oh yes," the old man said. "They would have preferred to lock me up, I'm sure. And they try. But every so often I manage to get away from them. For example, I told the story to you three detectives."

Franks looked at Danny, who was beaming, and grinned.

"You're very smart," Danny said.

"I *did* win a Nobel Prize," Franks concluded.

24. "Twenty years ago a woman came into my life who was fun, sexy, alive, loving, a ton of laughs, and who worshipped me"

"Breakfast in bed, lover," Rosie said, bringing in a platter of French toast and placing it on his lap. "Molasses, right?"

"Right," he said, sitting up in bed.

He wore a white tee shirt with a pair of boxers. She wore a white tee shirt.

He said, "It's the middle of the night."

"It's five in the morning," Rosie said.

"I was planning on sleeping until seven and then getting up to see how Brian has been doing," he replied.

"I'm surprised that you're not with him," Rosie said.

He took a bite of French toast. Then he said, "Slightly burned."

"Like you like it."

"You have *some* memory," Donovan said.

"I remember the hard-ons you used to get at five in the morning."

He groaned, and he said, "Please, *please*. I'm confused enough as things are."

"I was just teasing you. I really don't want your body."

"In time. One day it will happen. Out of the blue. Bang."

"You don't set the rules," Rosie said.

"And neither do you," he replied. "My days of having my life run by women are way fucking over."

He ate some more French toast. "This is really good." He took a sip of coffee. "This too," he added.

202

"Thank you," she replied. "So why are you here eating the breakfast I made for you instead of being out chasing bad guys with Brian Moskowitz?"

He reached over and took her hand. Then he said, "Because he doesn't need me to check the records of the Ford Motor Company, Mercury Division, and to prowl up and down Amsterdam and Saint Nicholas Avenues looking for dingy places that are quiet as a tomb. He has a whole department now, my old department. I trained them very well. Moreover he has your son—our son—helping him. He can wrap this up on his own."

"And you?" she asked.

"I'm tired. I feel old. Like Leonard Cohen said, 'I'm tired of this war. I want the kind of life I had before.' "

"You said you wanted to get up and call Brian," she said.

"Simple curiosity. After I satisfy that, I mean to walk up to the Starbucks that used to be the Riley's saloon where you and I met. I mean to have a cup of coffee and read the *Times* like I used to. Then I think I'll come home and go back to sleep."

"I'll be sleeping," she said.

"I'll be quiet," Donovan promised.

She slipped under the covers and slid over next to him and rested her head on his shoulder.

"You'll get molasses on your cheek."

"TFB," she replied.

He was calm, quiet, thinking, for a moment. Then amidst a yawn he said, "I wonder how Gregorio Paz got involved in this. Why was a Latino janitor prowling around the tunnels, looking for clues about the Mercury Building?"

"Ask Brian," she replied.

"That's the only piece of this puzzle that bothers me," Donovan said. "The fact that Riverside would heap its shit on the neighboring community is business as usual, I'm afraid. You know—town versus clowns."

She chortled.

"But Gregorio Paz—what the hell were you up to? You were too young to have remembered the nuclear terrors of the Cold War. You didn't have a personal stake that I can think of. What was it, righteous outrage over the nukes-in-Harlem thing?"

"Lieutenant Wonderful will straighten it out. Have a good sleep, read the paper, and then get back to finding McGowan."

"If he's even still alive," Donovan said.

He finished his breakfast, then reached over and down and left the platter on the floor.

"Thanks again," he said.

She rolled away from him like he did to her the previous night, then said, "My sister will be out of my apartment in two weeks. Will you help me to move?"

"Sure."

"We can see each other a lot. Order Chinese and sit up and talk. Like we did before I moved in here twenty years ago. We can take time to sort all this out. To sort *us* out."

He gave her a "Mmm hmm," then said, "I have something for you. A special credit card."

"I heard about that. I don't want it."

"You might need help with the rent," he said.

"If I lose my job at the Rosa Blanca maybe I'll take you up on it. In the meantime, take your money and shove it. I hate rich people."

Smiling, he said, "I think we're gonna be fine."

"You can pay for the Chinese, too," she said. "Now shut up and let me sleep."

He did that, rolled away from her, and in time they fell asleep, their bottoms touching, same as in the old days.

"Ah, the customary fate of dingy old tombs that are too far from midtown to enter the high-end real estate market," Donovan said. "They become parking lots."

"Why are you here?" Mosko asked, nonetheless sipping at the Starbucks that Donovan had brought him.

"I had nothing better to do. Besides, now that you're full time on the Mercury issue, I took an interest in Paz."

"He's really why I'm here today, and you fucking know it. I just need to clarify the Mercury thing. And there's the chance that McGowan's body will turn up in the middle of it."

"I hope not," Donovan said. "For one thing, he's the best hope I've found yet to help Danny. For another, I kinda like the sonofabitch, taking up arms against an injustice."

The two friends were quiet for a time, watching crime-scene technicians wander around the parking lot, on a corner of St. Nicholas Avenue, Geiger counters in hand.

"I'm never gonna arrest anyone for this," Mosko said.

"Probably not," Donovan agreed.

"What, a fifty-year-old crime with no body? A twenty-year-old coverup? This is one of those cases where the DA comes in and tells me what I can do."

"Prosecutorial discretion," Donovan said.

"Without a body, I'm dead," Mosko said.

"You can turn it into a public relations nightmare for Riverside University, and you may have to settle for that."

"It's something, I guess," Mosko said.

Then he waved at Bonaci, yelling, "Hey Howard, what's up?"

"What's up about what?" Bonaci yelled back.

Donovan said to Mosko, "Howard was nicer when he worked for me. What did you do, cut down on his overtime?"

"Ah, Howard is just worried about what he'll do when he retires next year. He's getting cranky."

Mosko aimed his mouth at Bonaci again, and yelled, "What do you fucking think I'm asking about? The daily number, that's what. *Qué es el número?*"

"Background radiation," Bonaci replied. "Just background, same as everywhere else."

"Oh balls," Mosko said to the Captain. Then to Bonaci, he yelled, "Okay, Howard, on to the next site—Amsterdam and one two seven."

"What's that?" Donovan asked.

"The last of the three old Mercury dealerships that I was able to find out about. Those records are *way* before computers. From what I can tell, they're way before microfiche."

"Speaking of years, how many has Howard put in?"

"Twenty, twenty-five. Why do you ask?"

"I don't know," Donovan said. "Maybe it's just that retirement has been on my mind lately. What did Howard do before he became a cop?"

Mosko wound up and yelled again, "Yo, Howard, Bill wants to know what you did before you became a cop."

"I played piano in a whorehouse," Bonaci yelled back.

"Things have gone all to hell since I left," Donovan said.

"What did you *do*, Howard?" Mosko asked again.

"Army."

"Doing what?"

"Sniper."

"Bullshit!" Mosko yelled.

Said Bonaci, "It's true, and I'm gonna start shooting if you don't leave me alone."

"I think it *is* true," Donovan said. "I kind of remember."

"He doesn't seem like the type. Mister Science."

"You never know what strange sort of gigs guys had before they got the calling," Donovan said. "I could have been a priest."

"Bull*shit*," Mosko said.

"It's true, man. When I was in eighth grade and about to be spat out of Saint Dominic's, the head nun . . . headmistress . . . penguin-in-command . . . the title eludes me . . . took me aside and told me that she had a visitation from God the night before."

Mosko yawned.

Donovan continued, "He came to her in her room. It happens, you know. I had a visitation myself last night. This one brought French toast."

"You and *women*," Mosko muttered.

"The nun said that God told her that I had an avocado . . . a vocation, I mean . . . that's kind of like a subpoena . . . to become a priest, and if I denied my vocation I was condemning myself, and her, to hell."

"Talk about shooting the messenger. What did you do?"

"I said, 'To hell with you,' and became a cop instead," Donovan said.

Bonaci and his crew of forensics detectives were decamping and about to move to the next location.

"We're heading over to Amsterdam," Mosko said. "Want to come?"

Donovan nodded. "I got nothing else to do," he said.

"I enjoy *your* company too. We'll hang out and go to lunch like the old days. What are you in the mood for?"

"Chinese," Donovan said.

"Awesome."

Donovan said, "I've made my peace with the Church and have even gone to a mass or two. Saint Pat's, the noon mass. Genuflected. Crossed myself. The whole nine yards. I guess I never told you."

"I guess you didn't," Mosko replied.

"Those days I just talked about were long ago in another era and people treated one another differently then, with kids who had to be beat the shit out of and threats of burning in hell and bombs that burn whole cities in hell."

He sucked in his breath and said, "I got okay with the Church. Now I got to get myself okay with women."

"This is about Rosie," Mosko said.

"Twenty years ago a woman came into my life who was fun, sexy, alive, loving, a ton of laughs, and who worshipped me. And I pushed her away because I just didn't get why she would want to be with a man who was drinking himself to death when he wasn't getting shot at."

There was silence between them, and for a nanosecond Mosko leaned toward his friend as if to administer a hug. Then he thought better of it, men could be watching, and Canarsie kicked in and he punched Donovan on the shoulder and said, "You ain't a young man no more."

"No, I ain't," Donovan agreed.

"Go get 'er," Mosko said.

"So it *is* Rosie, then," Marcie said. "I heard that she was back."

"Danny," Donovan said. "He ratted me out."

"What do you expect? You're his father. I'm his mother. Are you having sex with her?"

"First thing, no," he said. "Second thing, it's none of your business. You keep out of my private life and I'll keep out of yours."

"She's living with you," Marcie said. "That's fast, even for you. Even for a man your age."

Donovan bristled but controlled himself. "She's staying there until her own place is ready," Donovan said. "And that's all I'm saying."

She sniffed, then said, "You don't have to say any more."

"Who have *you* been seeing on all those long nights 'working late.' " He made quotation marks in the air with his fingers.

"Stay out of *my* personal life," she said.

The kettle was making a strange sort of noise. Donovan thought it was making music. He listened more closely. It was definitely music, and moreover the tune was "I Am Woman."

He smiled. "I dig the anger," he said.

Mistaking his sarcasm for a compliment, she said, "I got it at Bed, Bath and Beyond. It was only a hundred-fifty. You ought to get one."

"Do they have a model that plays 'Born to Run'?" he asked.

"I don't think so. Do you want coffee?"

He shook his head. "Not at night. Tea will do."

"You're not drinking?"

"Not at the moment," he said.

As Marcie poured him a cup of Darjeeling, she said, "I guess you're serious about separating."

He said that he was.

"I drew up some papers," she said. She put his cup in front of him and hers at her side of the table, which was as far from him as possible. "Want sugar?"

"Yeah."

She pushed it to him.

"It's a standard separation agreement. It's based on what you and I talked about. You don't have anything to worry about, but I suggest that you run it by a lawyer anyway."

"I will," he said.

"Who, someone with a storefront law practice on Broadway?"

He shrugged. "You said I don't have anything to worry about. So I won't. You're honest."

Marcie stirred her tea with a slender silver spoon, and for a moment stared at the swirling liquid.

"What happened?" she asked.

Donovan felt that her voice had come down a foot or two from the height of its anger.

"About us?" he asked.

"Yes."

"Too much past," he said. "Not enough present."

"We were good once," she said.

"We were *very* good," he replied.

"Is it Daniel?" she asked.

He asked what she meant.

"Eight out of ten couples who have children with issues break up," Marcie replied.

"You know that's not it."

"He's flawed."

"So am I. So is everyone I know. I like flaws. Look at my friends."

She kind of rolled her eyes, then shook off the gesture as soon as he noticed. Still, Marcie said, "They're not my people, William, and I've never quite accepted that they're yours."

"You once called them 'the scum of the earth.' "

"That was too strong and I apologize," Marcie replied.

He said, "They're the salt of the earth."

"They're drunks and janitors. And gamblers and extortionists."

"I don't know any extortionists," Donovan said.

"Petty mafia thugs and park litter picker uppers," she added.

"I haven't seen Picciotto in years and Jake is retired. Look, lighten up on them. What are your clients in the Bronx public defender's office, White House counsels and other Republican white-collar criminals?"

Irritated, she said, "My family is Democratic and you know it."

Donovan blew a little burst of air into his tea, making a dimple. Then he remembered how he splattered coffee on his face doing something like that the last time they were together. He stopped and put down the cup.

"Thanks for making it possible for me to retire and go after finding a cure for Danny," he said.

"Thank you for giving up everything for your son," she sighed, and reached across the table and bounced her middle finger on his upturned palm.

And then she added, "Including me," turning over her hand with the middle finger extended, and waving it in his face.

25. SLOW DEATH SPRINKLED
WITH OCCASIONAL LAUGHS

"What do you think of sopaipillas?" Donovan asked as he locked the front door of the Rose Blanca and drew the blind. It was four in the morning and they were closing up.

"*Mi abuela* made them. They're too sweet, sickly," Rosie replied. "Even as a little girl I hated them. Why do you ask?"

"Patrick McGowan liked sopaipillas."

"Maybe they killed him and that's why you can't find him," she said.

"The place down the block makes them," Donovan said.

"So does everyone," Rosie said.

"Not twenty years ago. Twenty years ago only the place down the block sold them in this neighborhood."

Rosie twisted and pushed the cork back into a bottle of Loughlin Vineyards merlot, then put it in its place on the bar.

"Who told you this?" she asked.

"Our kid," he replied.

"Lewis? Really? You asked him to do something for you? Oh, right. You mentioned." She was beaming. "He did a good job?"

"Lewis did a *great* job," Donovan replied.

"Want a drink?" she asked. "We'll celebrate his doing a great job for you."

Donovan shook his head.

"You didn't drink anything today or yesterday. On the wagon again?"

"No, just tired of having my tummy hurt. It really *is* a toxin, you know."

She knew. "Good now and then, though."

"Yeah, well, we can go out to dinner sometime, you know, share a bottle of wine."

"Yeah?" She smiled broadly. "You want to do that?"

"Absolutely," he replied, smiling back.

"Where do you want to go?"

"You pick," he said.

"No, you," she said.

He thought for a bit, ten or twelve seconds, all the time it took, and then he said, "Terrace. Remember Terrace?"

"Who could forget? After you got out of the hospital, to celebrate, remember. That guy shot at you with a shotgun while you were crawling down the storm drain under Riverside Park and you survived it. How many pellets did they take out of you, one hundred and nineteen?"

"About that. No. It was one hundred and two."

"Jefferson had them mounted in a frame and hung it over his desk," she added.

"I'll have to look him up one of these days," Donovan said.

Impulsively he reached across the bar and touched her hand, the back of her hand, just briefly, fingertips really, and they were pointed down.

She smiled at him again, a bit quizzically this time, and asked, "What is it with you tonight?"

"What's nothing with me," he said back.

"No. There's something with you. You're up to something."

He pulled his hand back. "Forget it," he said.

She took his hand and pulled it back to her side of the bar. She squeezed his hand. Then she pulled it back and smiled impishly.

"What *is* it, William?" she asked.

"Nothing, okay, nothing," he said. "I was just trying to be neighborly, that's all."

"It would *kill* you to say that you liked me, wouldn't it," she said.

"I *don't* like you."

"Come around behind the bar and help me clean up, neighbor."

He got off the barstool, and as he did so, he said, "I'm just going back there to help. I'm not going to work in a bar."

Rosie smiled and said, "Shut up and get your ass back here."

He shut up and got his ass back there, and as soon as he did she gave him an exaggerated kiss on the cheek.

"Cut it out," he snapped.

"You forgot to take your medication this morning, didn't you?" she said.

"I'm already sorry I tried to be nice," he replied.

She tossed a bar towel into his face. He caught it, and she said, "Dust off the bottles on the bottom row and make sure the labels are facing outward."

"What?" he laughed. " 'Make sure the labels are facing outward?' What is this, Sardi's? The guys you serve in here don't care if there are labels at *all.*"

"I'm trying to upgrade this dump," she said, handing him a bottle of apricot brandy to wipe off. He did so.

She continued, "I want it *cleaned up.* It feels so unhealthy in here."

"It's a goddam *bar,*" he said. "Health isn't what people come here for, all the sincere expressions of wellness they bellow at one another notwithstanding. What they come for is slow death sprinkled with occasional laughs."

"You're such a fucking delight," she said, yanking his chin in her direction and planting one on his lips.

"Wipe the bottles," he said. "I know—let's do it in alphabetical order, front to back. You take the high row and I'll take the low row and I'll be in vodka before you."

She gave him a long, distressed look, and shook her head. Then she turned away and whispered, to a bottle of Irish whiskey as it turned out, "I must be out of my mind."

Donovan smiled.

Then she said, "I can't work here if it's not cleaned up. This place has a history of wearing out owners."

"How so?" Donovan asked.

"Remember what you used to say about that place on a Hundred and Sixth that kept going out of business?"

Donovan remembered.

"It was a grocery. That went out of business. It was a ninety-nine cents store. That went out of business. It was—"

"I *remember*," he said.

"It was never the same thing for five years straight. You used to say—"

"That it was built on an Indian burial ground," Donovan said. "The land is jinxed."

"Same here," she said. "The last owner sold it after seven years and moved into a nursing home. Jinxed. Same thing with the guy before him. Got sick. Went to Florida to try his luck with the alligators. The place is jinxed. Indian burial ground."

Working side by side, they moved down the row of bottles, wiping off each in turn. She kept close to him, and now and again their hips touched. Once she hip-butted him in one direction, and then he hip-butted her back.

At the back end of the bar when they were done cleaning, she took his towel and gave it a little, teasing flip in the direction of his face. That was when he turned her to him and took the towels, both of them, and threw them over his shoulder into the back room.

He slipped the fingers of both hands under her belt and

pulled her to him and touched his lips to hers ever so lightly.

Her wide eyes met his, and he took her tee shirt by the bottom and pulled up and peeled it off her, and threw it into the back room with the towels.

"Downstairs," she said.

"It seems like almost yesterday," she said, playing with his chest hair as he lay on his back looking up through the canyon of beer kegs and bottles that rose around them in the nook they found against one wall.

"We didn't knock over the kegs this time," he said.

"Tomorrow. I miss the crash and the beer shower."

"I was thinking—" he said.

"Don't," she told him.

"Why?"

"You'll break the spell," she said, nuzzling into the warmth of his neck.

"Not a chance," he replied. "Not this time."

She made an "mmmmm" sort of sound, then was quiet for a moment, then said, "I'm still moving into my own place."

"I know."

"It's best," she said.

"I agree," he said.

"Don't agree with me so fast," she teased.

"What I was going to say before was that you have a lot more stuff now than you did before—"

"Yeah. In those days I owned a pair of jeans and a tee shirt, and you ripped that one off me too."

"Your apartment is so small. Leave some things at my house."

"Yeah? It's okay for me to do that?"

"Of course," he said. "Your closet is still there."

"It's not filled with your wife's shit? What was her name again?"

216

"Dunno," Donovan said.

"She took everything with her?" Rosie asked.

He nodded.

"Except your soul," Rosie said. "You hung onto that for me."

He smiled. "For Danny," he said. "But you can use it on alternate weekends."

"Do you think Danny will like me?"

"Absolutely," Donovan replied. "It may be touch and go at first, but he'll come around. He's a solid kid."

He shifted his weight a bit, then grumbled, then tried to stretch. The mattress that the bartenders kept there for naps was paper thin and hard against the cold, age-worn concrete that smelled of the decades.

"Are you okay, honey?" she asked. She unwrapped herself from around him so he could stretch. Then she sat up.

"Yeah. I'm just a bit rusty when it comes to fucking in bar-room basements."

"You'll get used to it. Especially after we get it cleaned up."

"We?" he asked.

She said " 'We' as in you and me," she said.

Donovan took a long and despairing look around and said, "This place, *this* place is dingy and old, dark as a tomb."

"You have no idea. It smells of oil from the furnace and—"

"The furnace is gas," he said. "But yeah, I noticed the oil smell too."

"And the water pipes vibrate when I run the water. Like that one over there."

She pointed at an ancient water pipe that rose up along one wall to disappear through the ceiling.

She continued, "I turn on the cold water upstairs and it vibrates. Not all the time, just when I have the water running fast."

"So run the water slow," he replied, imitating Henny Young-man.

"William," she said. "I have to come down here and there's this old wadded up piece of paper that someone stuck in there between the pipe and the wall ages ago like in prehistory but eventually it works its way out. I put it back in the other night but it vibrated out again. Roll over and put it back."

" 'Roll over and put it back.' " He grumbled as he did it.

The paper was indeed ancient and it was yellowing too. All that kept it from rotting away was that at some point in its wretched history it had become soaked with oil. It had been folded over many times until it seemed like thick cardboard. "I think you've uncovered a new Dead Sea scroll," he said.

"What are you talking about?" she asked, pushing her hair back behind her shoulders and straightening it with her fingers.

"What the hell *is* this?" he asked.

Donovan unfolded it and peered at it in the dim light, and then his brow furrowed and he sat up straighter. The hair stood up on the back of his neck, or so he felt anyway. It did the same around his temples and the skin on his forehead went tight as a drum.

He looked at the paper and thought back then to when he first saw the facade of the Rosa Blanca and its Roman arch of red brick, bleached by decades of blinding afternoon sun, that soared over what once was a garage entrance. There were bug-gies there once, a hundred years before, and then cars, and then . . .

Rosie saw his fear and anger and put a hand on his shoulder and asked, "What is it, honey?"

"A new Dead Sea scroll," he said, his voice beginning to tremble.

"What!"

"We gotta get out of here!" he said, scrambling to his feet

and pulling her up.

"*William?*"

"Put your clothes on. We gotta go!"

"What *is* it?"

"A receipt from the West Side Mercury Automobile Company, 53909 Broadway."

"That's this address," she said.

"I know. This says, 'Repair of clutch, 1939 Mercury Eight, black, $115'. It's dated December 14, 1941, the year that Mercury went out of production so they could make tanks."

She looked at him, speechless, not knowing what to think.

He said, almost yelling, "Grab your clothes. This basement is dangerous."

"Honey?"

"This building is 'Mercury'! This is where Franks did the isotope separation during the war. This is what Gregorio Paz was looking for in the records of Riverside University when he got killed. He was looking for proof that would take them down."

"We just found it," she said.

"No wonder the old owners got sick. It's radioactive. Come on, we gotta go!"

26. "It put a better head on the beer"

"Never let it be said that your dad doesn't know how to throw a party," Mosko said, placing a hand on Danny's shoulder as they watched the seemingly hundreds of local, state, and federal vehicles that, lights flashing and radios cackling, choked just about the entirety of Upper Manhattan. "You shoulda been there for New Year's Eve in Times Square when your dad and mom got married." Then he said, under his breath, "Come to think of it, you nearly were."

The Rosa Blanca was bathed in crime-scene light. Officials in uniforms mingled with technicians wearing what looked like space suits. Everyone who wasn't in a suit or a uniform was carrying an electronic device of one sort of another. Everything beeped and flashed.

Above were helicopters both civilian and official. Crowds were held back by a sea of blue uniforms. Everyone with a window was looking out of it, and half of *those* were using cell phones to take pictures. Danny would later inform his father that, within an hour of the news getting out that atomic bomb radiation had been discovered in the basement of a West Harlem bar, three blogs were created just to discuss it.

Standing on the other side of Danny, Donovan looked up heavenward and sighed.

Seeing this, Mosko said, "Wait—I know what you're going to say. 'I am become Death, the destroyer of worlds.' "

"I was going to say that the Goodyear Blimp has arrived,"

Donovan replied.

Rosie squeezed his arm and said, "I'm out of a job."

In one silent, seamless movement, Donovan slipped the American Express card out of his back pocket and into her back pocket, patting her butt as he did so. "Thanks, hon," she said, and rested her cheek on his shoulder.

Danny said, "Wow, Dad, did *you* do all this?"

"*We* did," Donovan replied. "All of us. You, me, Lewis, Rosie, Uncle Brian, all of us."

"Plus Marlowe and Jake," Rosie added.

"And Duke," Donovan said. "Poor Duke. He's the only one in the picture from the Middle East, and Homeland Security will be all over him like dirty on a duck. Someone ought to warn him to lose the toy gun and burn any records he may be stupid enough to have kept."

Then Donovan added, "And *you*, Mary O'Connor, my cousin from Ireland, you helped too."

She was hovering behind the Beast, her fingers touching Danny's shoulders.

"Where's Lewis?" Rosie asked, looking around the many unfamiliar faces that crowded inside the police lines in and around her.

"Maybe he doesn't have all the right passes," Donovan said, shaking the half-dozen or more security badges that hung from as many lanyards looped around his neck.

"He has them," Mosko said.

"Then where is he?" Donovan asked.

Rosie said, "Yeah, where's my baby?"

"How should I know?" Mosko grumbled.

"He *works* for you," Donovan said.

"Yeah, well, I worked with you for ten or fifteen goddam years and never knew where you were at any given moment."

"That's different," Donovan said.

"How so?" Mosko asked.

"I was the boss."

"And now *I'm* the boss and I say what goes, and if your kid feels like taking off for half an hour to get a slice and a Coke I'll deal with it. He's doing a hell of a job. Did I tell you I was thinking of requesting his services full time?"

"What?" Donovan asked.

"What yourself," Mosko said. "Is your hearing going too?"

"You want Lewis to work for you?" Donovan asked.

"That's better," Mosko said. "If you tilt your head so the good ear is aimed in my direction—"

"Lewis in the Department of Special Investigations?" Rosie said, astonished and pleased. "You want *another* Donovan after all this time?"

"Yeah," Mosko replied. "I'd like to beat up on a Donovan for a change. It's way overdue. Where the fuck is Officer Rodriguez?" Mosko looked around and saw nothing but law enforcement officials who had more power than him and bigger guns, too.

"This sucks," he said.

There occurred a generic disruption in the direction of the campus entrance. In trying to get a clear line of sight to its signal relay, an Eyewitness News location truck had snagged the power line leading to the journalism building and created a First Amendment crisis. Persons with varying degrees of authority were yelling and waving their arms while the neighbors snapped cell phone photos and the bloggers fulminated.

Another disturbance, this one off by where the yellow crime-scene tape—and the blue FBI tape *and* the orange Homeland Security tape—caught their attention.

"Lewis," Donovan said, as the young patrolmen bullied his way past two Fed suits.

"Wazzup, bro'?" Mosko asked.

"We gotta talk," Lewis said, out of breath.

"Lemme hear it," Mosko said. "I know, the pizza joint got no anchovies."

The young man tried to laugh and couldn't.

"Lewis, what's the matter?" Donovan asked.

"Yeah, are you okay?" Rosie asked.

"I'm . . . I'm fine. I'm just a little out of breath. Look, you guys—Dad, Lieutenant—you have to come with me."

"What is it?" Mosko asked.

"I don't want to tell you," Lewis said. "You got to hear it yourself."

"Lewis?" Donovan asked.

"Please . . . come with me."

Donovan and Rosie exchanged glances, and then the captain leaned over and whispered into Danny's ear, "I have to go do something. Are you okay staying here with Mary and Rosie?"

"Sure," Danny answered. "This is fun."

"I won't be long," Donovan said. "In the meantime, make sure these women don't get into any trouble, okay?"

"Okay!" the boy replied, and then went back to watching the show.

As Lewis pushed his way back through the crowd, still out of breath, and also looking as if his senses were tingling, Donovan and Mosko followed behind.

"What do you think he's up to?" Mosko asked.

Donovan shrugged. "He works for *you.*"

"And can be as hard to read as you. It's like my wife says, 'The apple doesn't fall far from the tree.' "

"Lewis!" Donovan yelled.

His son didn't look back, but gestured for them to keep following.

Once they got past the hubbub of officials and spectators, the going was smoother. What stood in their way was the infrastructure of news coverage—remote trucks with high telescoping antennae capped with satellite disks and the cables that snaked along the sidewalks and street. Drivers stood by their expensive news vans while generators hummed in the business of powering electronic journalism.

Sitting on a bench in the Broadway mall was a young woman tapping away on a notebook. Donovan would before too long come to know—from Danny, again—that she was a blogger whose specialty was minutia of TV remote trucks.

Neighborhood people and shopkeepers loitered about, as did scores of Riverside University students, many of them talking on cell phones or taking pictures of other students talking on cell phones, and the occasional homeless man or woman who suddenly were given something new to think about.

"Where the fuck are we going?" Mosko yelled at his young colleague.

"Just follow me, okay?" Lewis said, hurrying them down a side street away from the fuss. Several doors in the direction of Amsterdam Avenue was a tiny shop that carried the name Pacifico's Grocery.

"In here?" Donovan asked, catching up.

"In here."

"This where the sopaipillas live?" Mosko asked.

"You got it," Lewis said. "Want some?"

"No," Donovan and Mosko said, more or less in unison.

Several customers reached and squirmed around one another, picking at the shelves of bottles, cans, bags, and boxes, only about half of them Latino specialties.

"Assimilation," Donovan said. "Very retro."

"Everyone else wants to be ethnic these days," Mosko said.

Lewis led the way through the shop, nodding to and thanking the elderly woman at the counter. He took his father and boss into the back room, which was half storage area and half living room. There was a broken-down old rusty bed frame atop which sat a surprisingly new single mattress. A small color TV showed the fuss a few blocks away. It sat atop a card table that swayed gently with the movement of the hands and arms of an elderly, white-haired man, who was playing solitaire.

"Okay," Mosko said, "whaddya got?"

"You said I should go on my own—act on my own instincts," Lewis said. "So I did. I went through the files that we pulled and never looked at closely because you guys were out chasing nukes. I put a few things together and here we are."

He motioned for Mosko and Donovan to shake hands with the old man.

Lewis said, "This is my friend Pacifico."

"*Hola,*" said Donovan.

"I speak English," the man said.

Mosko smiled. "How ya doin'?" he said, pumping the old man's hand.

The captain said "Bill Donovan" and also shook hands.

"I met Pacifico two hours ago," Lewis said. "He has an interesting story."

"What?" Mosko asked.

The old man put down his cards. He stared at Donovan. He looked back and forth from Donovan to Lewis. And then he laughed, a good hearty laugh.

"What?" Donovan asked.

"You," Pacifico said to Lewis. "You have his eyes. And the forehead, but especially the eyes. And the eyes never lie."

"Whose eyes?" Donovan asked.

"Yours," the old man said. "*Usted es su padre.*"

Lewis said "Yes, this is my father, Captain Donovan—"

"*Retired* Captain Donovan," Mosko said.

"You're *americano,*" Pacifico said.

Lewis joined the old man in laughing, and then the young

225

officer said, "Wait 'til you hear this. You're gonna love it."

"Not if we don't hear it fucking *now*," Mosko said.

"I *knew* the young man," Pacifico said.

Mosko said "You don't mean—"

"He knew Paz, boss," Lewis said.

"Okay," Mosko said, apparently unsure if that was big enough news to drag them on this mystery mission down a side street off Broadway. Other persons who knew the victim had been spoken to, with no result worth mentioning.

"There's more, isn't there?" Donovan said.

"Oh yeah," Lewis said.

Smiling, the old man said, *"Su padre era americano."*

"What?"

"His father was American too."

This took two or three seconds to register, and then Donovan looked at the old man and asked, "What did you say?"

Pacifico said, "Gregorio Paz—his father was a gringo."

Donovan was about to say something, then didn't say anything, and then he said, *"His* father . . . no!"

"That's right," Lewis said.

"Holy fucking shit."

Lewis said, "I checked what Pacifico told me against the birth records. Paz was McGowan's son. Sorry, Dad, this means that McGowan is almost certainly dead."

"And Paz was out to track down the killer," Mosko said.

"After McGowan disappeared and the word was out that he had been murdered, the mother took her son home, to get him away from the life her family had made in America," Lewis said. "But eventually the son came back looking for his father's killer and to exact revenge."

"And found the killer, apparently," Donovan said.

Said Pacifico, "Paz was asking everyone at the university what happened to his father. And one day he told me he thought there was someone who would help him, a man who worked there."

"And we know who that is, don't we," Donovan said.

"I'll bet the man arranged to meet him in the Hub," Mosko said.

Lewis nodded and handed Mosko a small evidence bag. The lieutenant took it, held it by a corner, and peered at the little cash register receipt on which was faint lettering.

"This is one of the papers you guys found near the vic's body. You thought it had nothing on it. But while you were out chasing nukes, Bonaci's lab wizards managed to bring out the lettering. I asked him what they found, and you know what he said?"

"He told you to fuck off," Donovan said.

"He said, 'It's the work address of a Latina cashier with a great ass.' Look at the address."

Donovan took the envelope and squinted at it. "A bean wagon on Hunt's Point Avenue," he replied. "The street that leads from the subway to the Hunt's Point Meat Market."

Mosko said, "How about you and I tag along with Officer Rodriguez while he makes the arrest?"

Lewis beamed.

After they thanked the old man and bought a box of sopaipillas for the hell of it, the three of them left Pacifico's Grocery and went back to Broadway. They were walking downtown in search of a car that held more than Mosko's red Corvette and some backup, when Donovan felt a hand on his shoulder and an old and familiar voice say, "Tomorrow at six sharp."

Donovan turned to look into the face of his old pal and confidante Jake Nakima, whose grip was as firm as his smile was bittersweet.

"What's tomorrow at six?" he asked.

"The end-of-the-bar party," Jake said.

Donovan smiled and sighed simultaneously, which is not as easy as it sounds.

"Where?" he asked.

"This is the end, Bill."

"Of what?" Donovan asked, and then seeing Mosko's substantial form fading away downtown, yelled, "Hey, yo! Tragedy!"

Mosko turned, looked over his shoulder and saw Jake, and said, "What now?"

"I was just telling him that this is the end," Jake said.

"Of what?"

"The bar," Jake replied.

"You would rather sit and drink in radioactivity?" Mosko asked.

"We talked about it before. We think it puts a better head on the beer."

"And I keep hearing how weird Brooklyn is. We gotta go," Mosko said, beckoning Donovan and Lewis to follow.

"It's the end of everything," Jake said. "I've decided that it's time now."

"For a party?" Donovan asked.

"For my thirtieth mission," Jake replied, spiking his remark with a faint smile.

"I'll see you tomorrow at six," Donovan said, and Mosko and Lewis and he started off again.

"Riverside Avenue and Eighty-ninth," Jake called after him. "Across from your place."

"Where it all began," Donovan said.

If Thomas J. Keogh wondered why the cashier with the great bottom called him out of nowhere and asked him if he might stop by, he gave no indication. If he wondered why she suddenly disappeared after serving him coffee and a cinnamon cruller, he gave no indication of that either.

Nor did he appear to have the slightest awareness when Donovan and Mosko suddenly appeared to flank him at the otherwise empty luncheonette counter. Lewis stood behind them, and behind *him* were two other policemen.

"You're busted, asshole," Mosko said

Then Keogh whipped his head from one detective to the other, and maybe he reached for a weapon, and Donovan pressed the barrel of his old Smith & Wesson against his forehead.

Then Donovan hissed, "Go ahead . . . make my day."

"The captain and his girlfriend have been watching a lot of movies since he retired," Mosko explained.

"What's going on?" the fat man stammered.

"Take your gun out and hand it to me," Donovan said.

"Nice and slow," Mosko added.

"I don't get it," Keogh said.

"Yeah you do," Donovan replied. "Let's have the gun."

Keogh reached for his weapon and handed it over. Donovan took the clip out and stuck it in his pocket. Keogh's hands were shaking.

"Guys . . ."

"Here's how it happened," Donovan said. "A lot of cops have careers before they become cops. Howard Bonaci was a sniper in the army. I was a priest . . . well, I got offered the job. Lieutenant Wonderful here was the bouncer at the 2001 Disco in Brooklyn. You remember, John Travolta and *Saturday Night Fever.*"

"Bullshit," Mosko said. "It was CBGB, okay punk, not disco. Johnny Rotten and the Sex Pistols. You're not a cop anymore and don't have to get the facts straight, but try not to abuse the privilege."

Lewis snickered.

Donovan continued, "Here are the facts with *you*, Tom, as my friends in the NYPD gave them to me. Before you joined the police department you ran security at Riverside University. Then you were a cop for twenty years, and then you grabbed your pension and went back to Riverside."

"Because you had a reputation for solving tricky problems," Mosko said.

"In 1988 the problem was Patrick McGowan," Donovan said. "McGowan had become a big problem after tripping over the fact that our distinguished academicians had conducted uranium enrichment in Harlem so as not to endanger their precious students."

"And *that* is a problem," Mosko said.

"Then they tried to cover it up," Donovan said.

"Another problem," Mosko added. "You've read the crime stories coming out of Washington these days. They don't get you for the *crime*. They get you for the cover-up."

Keogh swiveled around so as to face his accusers. The effort of getting his belly around past the counter made him out of breath.

"You don't understand," Keogh said.

"Don't we?" Donovan said.

"What we understand is that someone at Riverside—Yeager, probably—asked you to take care of McGowan," Mosko said. "For the sake of argument, let's say that you didn't mean to kill him. But that's what happened, isn't it?"

Keogh said, "No, no, that never happened."

"Are you gonna keep saying that after we find the body?" Mosko said.

"I didn't kill McGowan."

"Fast forward twenty years," Donovan said. "You've just taken your twenty and retired from the force and are happily eating donuts in Hunt's Point. At this place, in fact. Trans-Fat

Express. What happens? It's Riverside University on the phone again."

"They got *another* problem," Mosko said.

"This time it's the son of the man you killed in 1988, come for revenge," Donovan said.

"I didn't kill McGowan," Keogh insisted.

"So you go back to work for Riverside," Mosko said. "For Yeager again, in fact . . . and you do the same thing. You killed the father. You killed the son."

"We've got the Holy Ghost in protective custody," Donovan said.

"Look at this, pal," Mosko said, dangling the little evidence bag in front of Keogh. "This is a cash register receipt from this palace. We found it next to Gregorio Paz's body. And guess what? It has your thumbprint on it."

"Who buys a *cruller* and keeps the receipt?" Donovan asked.

"You're under arrest for the murders of Patrick McGowan and Gregorio Paz," Mosko said. "Officer Rodriguez, would you do the honors?"

Lewis stepped around him and took Keogh by the arm to urge him to his feet.

"McGowan's not dead!" Keogh shouted.

Donovan waited until Lewis finished reading the man his rights, then said, "Horseshit."

"The last time I saw him he was getting onto a Greyhound on the lam from some bookie."

"Duke," Donovan said.

"Yeah, the Turk. McGowan was afraid of me and scared shit-less of the Turk, and so he wanted to disappear. The Turk told everyone he killed him, and apparently word eventually got to the son that his father was dead and Riverside was behind it."

"Where was the Greyhound headed?" Donovan asked.

"New Orleans, I think."

Donovan looked out on the street at the passing white trucks that seemingly all had the word "meat" in their company names. Then he said, "I must have gotten there too soon after the hurricane. Maybe it's still possible to find the records."

Keogh said, "I want a lawyer."

"Eat shit and die," Mosko said.

"I can help you," Keogh pleaded. "I can give you Yeager. His whole life is in that place. It goes, he goes. A hint of scandal, anything, he goes."

"Talk to the DA," Mosko said. "Work out your deal with him."

"Let's go, pal," Lewis said as he led Keogh to the other cops and, with them, to a waiting car.

Mosko looked around at the pots of coffee and the racks of donuts and said, "I'm stealing a jelly donut. What will you have?"

"Two tickets to N'awlins," Donovan said.

"Say what?"

"He went to N'awlins," Donovan said, looking out the window and addressing the meat trucks.

"He could be dead," Mosko said. "Keogh could have been telling the truth."

"McGowan is alive," Donovan insisted.

Said Mosko, "Who takes off for twenty years, leaving his infant son behind?"

And as he came to the end of his sentence, he tried to rail in the words, but they got out into the air nonetheless.

"He might not have known he had one," Donovan sighed. "I'm going after him."

Mosko grabbed himself a jelly donut and, while so doing, nailed a cinnamon cruller for his old friend. "I'm gonna miss you, bro'," Mosko said.

They walked out the door and watched as Keogh was driven off.

"You can find Danny and me in N'awlins," Donovan said. He took the cruller and bit off the end, then scowled at it and threw it at a passing meat truck. "I'll make sure you have the address. And I *will* come back. You need a hand again, you just call."

27. To the Grave

The smoke from grilled burgers and hot dogs and the salt air of early evening rose from the brace of barbeque grills set up on the grass on a hill that looked down on the Hudson. Above it was the rising hulk of the Soldiers and Sailors Monument. Above *that* was the ridiculously large, ridiculously inexpensive rent-controlled apartment that had been in the Donovan family for four generations.

They were all there, the whole cast of characters, more or less anyway. A special permit from the NYPD made possible just the sort of party routinely denied private individuals, and the Captain's old pals going back further than he would admit without duress sniffed out debauchery and pounced.

Donovan and Rosie walked down the path from the mall that separated the park from the avenue, Riverside, that had lent its name to a million West Side dreams and romances and to the university, way farther uptown, that had shattered so many dreams. They followed Lewis and Danny, with the older brother struggling to keep up with the Beast.

Mosko was already there, tending bar. He had put two coffee tables together and was lording over an array of beer and whiskey. Seeing the array, Donovan pulled Rosie over there, pointed at the bottles, and said, "These labels need to be facing out. You take the high row—"

"Oh fuck you, William," she said.

"If it ain't Gypsy Rose Bourbon," Mosko asked.

"Hey you," she said. "Take your feeble attempts at humor back to Brooklyn where failure is a way of life."

"Oh God," Mosko said, pointing, in sequence, at Donovan, Danny, and Rosie, "There are *three* of them and one is a chick."

"Wild Turkey," she said.

"You got it," he replied, and reached for the bottle and a plastic glass.

"I'll have a Bud," Donovan said.

"No you won't," Mosko replied.

Donovan made a growly sound. "I said—"

Mosko replied, "What'd they nail that guy in Albany for?"

"If he was working in Albany, I would say the charge was promulgating boredom," Donovan replied.

"No, seriously, the state attorney general."

"Using state employees to drive his wife around," Donovan said. "Now that the civics lesson is over, can I have my Bud?"

"Well, you better call and turn me in, 'cause I had cops driving around all day looking for this."

He pulled out a bottle of Turbodog, flipped off the cap, and handed it over.

"Where'd you get that?" an astonished Donovan asked.

"There's an exotic beer store in Yorktown," Mosko replied.

"Thanks!" Donovan said, taking a swig. "Colossal," he said.

From off behind the grill, the Captain heard George Kohler yell out, "We sold out. All the food is gone. I got nothing for you."

Rosie yelled back, "Yeah, well *you*, you can take your salmonella and feed it to the pigeons."

"Four hot dogs coming up," George replied.

There was a breeze up off the river, and young lovers playing Frisbee danced and leaped in a balletic *pas de disk*. Out on a peaceful river, four women in orange and blue crew uniforms rowed a shell on a southerly course, silent as seen from the picnic on the hill. A woman was speed walking, while a man jogged along pushing a baby in a jogging stroller. Assorted couples walked along hand in hand. Uptown a bit, also on the crest of the hill, a lone bagpiper serenaded the setting sun. It was the first day of summer.

The Donovan clan and Rosie ate, drank, and sat on a sheet spread out on the grass, Danny swinging down out of his chair to join them.

They sat for an hour while Donovan, fresh from another triumph that was spread across more headlines and secure in the knowledge that he was retiring at the peak of his form, shook the hands of a string of old-timer well-wishers.

"Good King William has returned to the site of his early victories," Rosie said, tossing in a kiss rapidly enough to ward off a flurry of obscenities.

Along came Charlie the janitor, still fixing pipes and installing locks after all those years. Harold the electrician who worked over at the Museum of Natural History showed up, long having lost the title Little Harold. He lost that a quarter century earlier when Donovan blew Big Harold to pieces in the train tunnel below Riverside Park, but not before accumulating 102 shotgun pellets. Roland Gomez showed as well. Now retired, he made his mark in Donovan's early career by being the Riverside Park worker who swept up the burned candles and decapitated chickens that were among the shards of the case that brought Donovan fame, 102 shotgun pellets, a dead killer beneath the park in which they now sat, Rosalie Rodriguez and, portentiously, Marcia Barnes.

A few other ghosts slid past, the sun made some threats about setting, and then came the sound of angry voices, a pleading voice, and, at last, a fearsome shove, the end result of which was Duke Dermirci landing in a heap at Donovan's feet.

Rosie and Danny lurched back, and she reached for him

protectively. But Mosko grinned and so did Donovan, who sprang to his feet to hurl a mighty hug on an old friend and partner who had left his life long ago, angrily, and of necessity.

"Deputy Chief Jefferson!" Donovan exclaimed, administering a second hug.

"Hey bro'," Jefferson said.

Mosko was on his feet too and so was Rosie, and Mary took over the job of protecting Danny from the emotion that out of nowhere detonated the energy in that piece of the planet.

"It's the man himself," Mosko said, and was about to give a hug of his own when Jefferson put his hand up and turned it into a handshake.

"Don't come near me with your four-hundred-and-fifty-pound bench presses," Jefferson said. "You'll wrinkle the fabric."

"Still the Brooks Brother suits," Donovan said, standing back to admire the fashion on the man who long before began a one-man crusade to demolish the notion that black men didn't dress well.

"No way, man, these are custom," Jefferson said, plucking proudly at the lapels.

On the ground, Duke grumbled to a sitting position and began to make speaking sounds when Jefferson motioned to a burly detective to move closer.

"Shut up, fool," Jefferson snapped.

Those in and around the party who were long accustomed to Duke being the height of fear were enjoying the hell out of seeing him laid low.

To Donovan, Jefferson said, "Damn. Captain William Donovan. *Retired* Captain Donovan, if my spies are correct."

"They are that," Donovan said.

Jefferson looked at Rosie and said, "And you too. You back for this party, or for *him?*"

"Both," she said, "and I forgive you for calling me his 'Chiquita Banana.' "

"You got some memory," Jefferson said. He added, "I hear that you being back means that High Yellow is gone."

Rosie nodded.

"Well, bless you. This is way overdue. Bill, I warned you about her and—"

"And I'd like you to meet my son Danny," Donovan said.

"Oh, *yeah*," Jefferson said. "I heard about you too. How you doing, Danny?"

"Good," the boy replied.

"Your old man and I used to work together," Jefferson said.

"Yeah."

"Your dad is a good man. You take good care of him."

Danny smiled a big smile.

Then Jefferson turned to Lewis and said, "I heard about you too."

They shook hands.

Jefferson indicated Mosko, grinned, and said, "If you ever get tired of working with this loser I want you to give me a call."

"Okay!" Lewis said, first giving Mosko a cautious look.

Donovan sucked in his breath, punched it out, and said, "Okay, man, did you come to say goodbye or to deliver a package?"

He pointed down at Duke, who the threats notwithstanding had managed to sit up.

Jefferson said, "If you recall, I used to pick up the garbage for you all the time. I picked up another piece."

"He grabbed me out of my car," Duke protested, earning himself a threatening look from the burly detective.

"I grabbed him out of the arms of Homeland Security," Jefferson said. "Someone ratted him out and he was about to be nabbed, but I got there first."

"He beat the shit out of me," Duke said.

"Not personally," Jefferson said. "My suit."

"Did he cuff you to the radiator in his office?" Donovan asked.

Confused, Duke said, "What, I . . . no."

Donovan grinned. "So you're ahead of the game. Here, stand up."

Jefferson indicated that it was all right, and Donovan helped the shattered man to his feet

"What did you try to do?"

"He ran," Jefferson said.

"Switching on your gene for pursuit," Donovan said, using a phrase he often used referring to himself. "Where were you going?"

"Albany," Duke said.

Laughing, Donovan said, "Why Albany?"

"It's boring. No one would think of looking for me there."

"Homeland Security would have found you," Jefferson said. "I saved your sorry ass."

"You call this 'saving'?" Duke exclaimed, showing his bruised face.

"Can you spell 'Guantanamo'?" Donovan asked.

Duke had no answer for that, so he rubbed his chin.

Jefferson said, "He said he helped you on something, so I thought I'd run him by you."

"He helped me on something," Donovan said. "I mean, he didn't and he did, but basically he did."

"Okay, so I'll have a few words with Bush's boys."

"I have a few words for them myself," Donovan said.

"I knew you would," Jefferson said.

He turned to his burly assistant and said, "Get him out of here. Cuff him to the radiator in my office until I can work this out."

As the perplexed man was led off, Donovan gave his old friend a good solid handclasp and said, "Do you want something to drink? Want a burger or something?"

"From *him?*" Jefferson looked at George, and was rewarded with an up-yours gesture.

"Feed it to the pigeons," Jefferson yelled.

"Come sit for a while," Donovan said. Then he thought better of it and said, "Right. Your suit."

"That's right. Anyway, I have to go uptown and play potentate up at the Rosa Blanca. The Feds are still going over that. Probably will be for a month. Tell me, what the hell was this bunch of honkies doing in West Harlem?"

He swept an arm around, indicating the partygoers.

"Wave of the future, man," Donovan said. "Walt Disney and white folks from Kansas taking over this city. They're everywhere. You better post guards around your house in the Harlem Historic District."

"Already have, bro'," Jefferson said.

Then he said goodbye to the others, and then he pulled Donovan and Mosko away from the crowd. Rosie tried to come with them, but Jefferson held up his hand and said, "Give us a minute, Chiquita."

Rosie made a face at him, but kept her distance.

"That thing with Marcie in Harlem," Donovan said.

"Ed James died, you know," Jefferson said.

"I didn't know that."

"Cancer. In Florida. It wasn't in the papers."

"I'm sorry," Donovan said.

"Me, too. But you know, that leaves the three of us who know what happened that day."

"What day?" Donovan said.

"That day in Harlem with Marcie."

"I don't remember no day in Harlem," Mosko said.

"Me either," Jefferson said.

They said goodbye again, and this time Jefferson let Mosko

hug him, and then Jefferson said, "To the grave."

"To the grave," Donovan replied.

28. Heart of Gold

"I like New Orleans," Donovan said. "It reminds me of the Village in the sixties. There's a nice kind of street vibe. I could live there."

"But you're not going to," Rosie said.

"No. This is my home. New York will always be my home."

"Thank God for that," she said.

It had gotten hot in the week or two that passed since Keogh was arrested and made a deal for leniency in return for giving up Yeager, the Riverside University official who was so frightened of losing all he had that he sanctioned and paid for a homicide.

"When I was down there the last time, I went into the dive that became world famous for staying open during the entire Katrina thing. They just refused to leave. Told the National Guard to fuck off when they tried to remove them. Six days. Maybe seven. They took an oil drum or something and held a rotisserie on the sidewalk."

"I saw it on TV."

"I felt that I had to have a beer there. You know what I found? There's a sign over the bar reading 'Ignore the Gunfire.' Now if that ain't my kind of place I don't have one."

He handed over a black plastic garbage bag stuffed with clothes. It had a strip of masking tape on it upon which she had printed "Summer."

"I don't like you making jokes about gunfire," she said.

"Don't worry. I'm not in the mood to get shot at anymore," he said.

Rosie stopped moving boxes and bags for a moment, for long enough to stretch.

"This used to be easier. Tell me, I've been busy getting ready to move and you've been off being a cop for the final time. What did Brian and you decide was the story with McGowan and Paz? I mean, the *final* story, Duke and everything."

"Riverside covered up the fact that their Nobel Prize winner contaminated a West Harlem building with radiation and made several subsequent owners sick and God knows what else. Riverside was afraid that if the news got out it would make them liable to criminal prosecution, lawsuits, and loss of funding."

"I saw on Court TV that it already has."

"The cover-up nearly succeeded, but for Patrick McGowan. Worried about the health of his *Xenopus*, he—"

"Say what?"

"African clawed frog."

"I *knew* that's what it was," she said.

Donovan continued, "He bought a Geiger counter and began prowling the underground. What set him off? Maybe he was having trouble keeping his stem cells alive and suspected that the problem lay down the tunnel, in Franks' lab. Maybe he had residual fear and anger from the nuclear scares of the Cold War. Maybe Marlowe's end-of-the-world party really stuck with him. Then one day he went right to the source and asked the great man himself. And there came a stunner—Franks owned up to "it," the famous "it." He told McGowan that the isotope separation was done in "the Mercury Building."

"They put all the radiation and the danger in Harlem," Rosie said.

"Where it was okay if a few locals were made ill. McGowan

243

began combing the records in search of the Mercury Building. He desperately wanted to find it."

"Why?"

"There's no way to tell," Donovan said. "It could have been sheer altruism. He could have wanted to blackmail the university into getting him more money for his stem-cell research. Maybe he was angry for what they did. Maybe he was just crazy."

"Then they drove him off, or killed him, or what?" she asked.

"It was probably a combination of things," Donovan said. "Yeager hired Keogh to threaten him. Duke actually *did* threaten him after he lost big time trying to get money to get away. Who knows. The point is that everyone thought he was dead, including his son. He may have felt it was best that way. So he got on a Greyhound headed for New Orleans, and Danny and I are going after him. I must have missed something when I tried a while ago. We'll see if we can pick up the trail there."

"And you don't think he's dead," she said.

"My gut reaction is that he's out there," Donovan said. "And we're going to find him."

Rosie tugged at the bottom of her tee shirt, pulling it out of her jeans and waving it around so the sweat on her tummy would dry. Then she walked around in a circle, again to get some air on her body.

"And Paz," she said. "Tell me the final resolution on Paz."

"I'm not sure exactly," Donovan said. He plucked his bottle of spring water from where he had perched it atop a fire hydrant and gave her a sip. Then he took one himself. "Brian thinks that he got the word from his father's old pals in the 'hood that his old man had been murdered and that Riverside and its anthill of tunnels had something to do with it."

"And he came looking for proof," Rosie said.

Nodding, Donovan said, "And that got Yeager to bring back Keogh to frighten another one off. But it got out of control, and

Keogh wound up killing him and leaving him to exsanguinate on the floor of the Hub, the center of the spoke of tunnels."

"Find another show, please. You've seen every *CSI* six times."

Donovan bridled, and said, "Hey, I used to drink with David Caruso right after he got out of Bishop Molloy in Queens. There was this Irish joint on Jamaica Avenue "

"No you didn't," she said. "You made that up." She pretended to take a slap at him. He pulled his head back.

"Yeah, you're right."

She said, "Hand me that box, would you?"

They got back to what they were doing, which was using the Dannymobile to move her into her old apartment. She had lived in Donovan's apartment for three weeks, and now it was time for her to go. A lot of her stuff remained behind at his place, as agreed, and in her old closet from the time they lived together.

They were taking boxes from the van and putting them onto a dolly on the sidewalk on 106th Street. Down on the corner, the store that sat atop an Indian burial ground had become a ninety-nine-cent store with a "going out of business" sign in the window.

He handed her a medium-sized box that once held Heinz ketchup, the ones where the bottles are upside down. The box now held kitchenware, if you could call it that, cheap tin or whatever people called tin in the twentieth century, battered with dents and bent handles.

"You had this stuff when we were together the first time," he said. "What's the matter, there've been no sales at Bed, Bath and Beyond in the past two decades?"

"Listen to yourself," she replied.

"You never throw anything out. You remind me of my mother. Are you still boiling water for coffee in a dented little stew pot instead of an official water-heater-upper with a whistle on it?"

She reached into the box, pulled it out, and waved it at him before putting it back. "It works, William. Don't fuck with success. Hand me the box."

"These days they make kettles that play 'Born to Run,' did you know that?"

"Hand me the box."

He did so.

"Worse things could happen to you, you know," she said. "You're lucky to have me back. *Sort* of have me back."

After six all-night talk fests with Chinese food and Loughlin Vineyards chardonnay, Donovan and Rosie agreed on their future—friends, best friends, and occasional perpetrators of mindless sex.

As she put it, "friends with privileges." Until, if and when, some better arrangement hopped the bus up Broadway and into their futures.

That was their decision. They shook on it. And then they exercised their privileges.

Now she said, "Gregorio Paz. Finish the story."

"Before he died he crawled down the tunnel to the basement of the library. Maybe it was by chance. Maybe he thought there would be someone smart enough to figure out what he meant when he said 'Mercury' as his dying word."

"He was right. He found someone."

"And that's the name of that tune," Donovan said.

Said Rosie, "I came to see you again because I was afraid that you would get killed or something and I would lose my last chance to see you again."

He said, "Despite my best efforts over five-plus decades, I remain alive."

"I know now that you'll go on forever. You and Danny."

"And Lewis," he said. "My sons."

"And me."

"And you," he replied.

He handed her another box, which he noted was packed with thongs, cutoffs, and bottles of Retin-Ox.

She saw it too, and smiled. "We do the best we can in life for as long as we got it."

"You got it, kid, you got it. I got back where I belong, this paradise . . ."

He swept an arm in the direction of the mall in the middle of Broadway, site of many parties for Donovan and his friends over the years. "There's the deck."

Two homeless men were engaged in a stare-off over who had claim to the shady bench, while a young man with a strange yellow backpack played Neil Young's "Heart of Gold" on a harmonica.

A black helicopter flew north over the river.

Beyond them another No. 104 bus rumbled uptown, having come all the way from the United Nations, along the Disneyfied theme park that 42nd Street in Times Square had come, and uptown and back to what used to be called, not without occasional affection, the ghetto.

Its exhaust blew the Wendy's wrappers back into the gutter and the hydraulic brakes made moms pull their children away from the curb.

"Family room," Rosie said.

Donovan cast a nod in the direction of the local Sabrett hot dog wagon. "There's the kitchen," he said. "Who needs townhouses?"

"Are we gonna make it together this time, in round two?" she asked.

He replied, "I don't know. There's a lot of past and not enough present. But anything is possible. This is New York." And the second he uttered this uncertainty he regretted it.

When a hint of sadness flittered across her eyes, he realized he had stepped in it *yet again,* probably got his privileges taken away indefinitely, and he smiled and said, "Yes. Danny and you and me and the rest of the gang are all gonna get well from here on. I know it now."

"Do you mean that?" Rosie asked.

"We'll deal with the past and work on the present." He enfolded her in his arms and kissed her on the top of the head where the blond hair kissed the grey hair, and then he said, "I'm home, kiddo, and I'm yours for as long as you want it."

Wiping away a nascent sniffle, she said, "I'm not sure if I want it," and then she sort of laughed.

Donovan thought to say something else, and then he couldn't think of anything to say and it was probably better to stay shut up anyway, so he turned to listen to the kid playing "Heart of Gold" and was quiet.

ABOUT THE AUTHOR

American author and critic **Michael Jahn** was born in Cincinnati and raised in Sayville, New York. Educated at Dowling College, Adelphi University, and Columbia University, he moved to New York City in 1966. Using the byline Mike Jahn, in 1968 he became the first rock critic of the *New York Times* and first full-time rock critic for any major daily newspaper.

The notoriety given him by his *Times* bylines allowed him to switch to writing fiction, and he eventually published about fifty novels and movie and TV adaptations, mostly as Michael Jahn. His first mystery novel, *The Quark Maneuver,* won an Edgar Award in 1978. In 1982 he began the series "The Bill Donovan Mysteries" with *Night Rituals.* As of 2008, he had published ten novels in the series, *Donovan & Son* being the most recent.